D0913140

ELSEWHERE

ELSEWHERE

WILLIAM PETER BLATTY

CEMETERY DANCE PUBLICATIONS

Baltimore

❖ **2009** ❖

Cemetery Dance Publications
132-B Industry Lane, Unit #7
Forest Hill, MD 21050

ISBN-13: 978-1-58767-083-1

Cover Photograph Copyright © 2009 by Bruce Haley
Interior Artwork Copyright © 2009 by Alex McVey
Interior Design by Kathryn Freeman

Printed in the U.S.A.

In loving memory of
Peter Vincent Galahad Blatty

Once I was afraid of dying. Now what I fear are the dead.

Why did I come to this place? Was it loneliness? Pride? The money? The creak of the floors, the color of the air, all things are a terror to me here. The house is bright, my companions amusing; why do I find myself thinking in whispers? Is it merely that the dark is coming on? I doubt it; I have touched the other side many times, it's my business. But this time it's different: something is wrong, something unfixable, like an ancient grief, like hell.

The rain has finally stopped, there's the sun, hate-red and breathing silent at the rim of the world. I ask why I'm frightened? Listen! Voices. Whispers. They're coming from the walls.

Inside them.

Jesus save me from this night!

From the Diary of Anna Trawley,
Tuesday, 8:22 p.m.

PART ONE

CHAPTER ONE

A PALE PINK TELEPHONE wedged at her chin, Joan Freeboard edgily stood at her desk while she rustled through message slips, frowning and impatient, as if searching for the one that would explain why she'd been born. A second line began to flash. She eyed it.

"Yeah, I know you already said you're coming," she scolded in a petulant, husky voice; in her accent one heard organ grinders strolling through the tenements, the flapping of wash hung out to dry upon a roof. "So what? You need constant reminding, Terry," she hounded. "You remember what night and what time?"

She listened, pursed her lips, then tossed the slips to her desk. "I knew it. Write it down:

Friday night at six o'clock. And remember, don't bring the freaking dogs!"

She punched into the flashing line.

"Yeah, Freeboard."

She wrinkled up her nose in distaste.

"Harry?"

Freeboard shifted her weight and fiddled with an earring, a southwestern dangle of stone and blue beads. Thirty-four, she wore short blond hair in bangs and had lost green eyes in a Kewpie doll face that masked a will with the grip of gravity. She lifted an incredulous eyebrow. "Co-list a contemporary in Greenwich, Harry? Are you out of your freaking *mind?* Ever since that cookbook lady bought a Tudor, all the yuppies ever want there is something 'authentic,' meaning dark and depressing and falling all to shit. Look, you go and get the cookbook lady to build herself a house made out of glass, something round or triangular or shaped like a saucer and looks like it probably *landed* in Greenwich and then maybe after that we can talk, okay? So what else? Make it quick would you please? I'm in a hurry."

A middle-aged secretary quietly entered, despondent, her hair in a bun, just divorced. Freeboard handed her the copy for an ad, mouthing *"Times."* The secretary nodded and drooped away. Freeboard watched her with pity and then spoke into the phone. "No, Thursday's bad for me, Harry," she said grimly. "How about never? Is never good for you?" She crashed the pink telephone down on its cradle. "Dumb, boring, arrogant shithead!" she told it. "I've already screwed you! Why in shit would you think I'd want to screw you *again?*"

She snatched up her jacket and purse from a chair, told the secretary "Take a long lunch today, Millie," and strode out into the windowed Trump Tower arcade and then out to Fifth Avenue and its bustle, its squalls of stalled traffic in shadowed May. From the curbside she hailed a Yellow Cab and got into it.

"Where to?"

Freeboard hesitated, staring straight ahead. Something had found her. What was it? Some vague premonition. Of what? And what had she dreamed last night? she wondered.

"Where we goin'?"

"Somewhere else," Freeboard murmured.

"Somewhere else?"

She came back, and her dimpled chin jutted up slightly, as if with a child's defiance and grit.

"Seven-seventy East River Drive," she commanded. The cab and her thoughts lurched forward into gridlock, into the patterned sleep of her life.

"This is it," she said assuredly half an hour later.

She was standing in a slowly ascending construction elevator with a couple from Hinsdale, Illinois, who were searching for a condo in Manhattan. Quiet, staring down at the elevator floor, they wore red hard hats over thoughtful expressions and hair that was white as the Arctic fox. Freeboard adjusted her own hard hat and finished, "You can't get newer than this."

The elfin elevator operator nodded. Stooped, middle-aged, looking older than his years, he wore a floppy and torn old gray wool sweater and was missing both his upper and lower front teeth. "Best views," he grunted gummily. "Yeah. Ya see everythin'— the Williamsboig Bridge, the whole river. Sly Stallone is gonna take a place here. I seen him yestiddy."

The building soared breathless above the East River. The couple wanted "new"; they had seen enough "old"—apartments for sale by their current occupants. "Why is it," the husband had grumbled, "that in all of these terribly expensive apartments, every room where a guest might go looks great, but you walk into any other room, like the kitchen, and the place looks like the embryo ward in *Alien.*" Across from the Museum of Natural History, the master bedroom of a luxury apartment had only a single illumination, a naked bulb suspended by a wire coiling down from a crumbling and smoke-stained ceiling; in another a shower stall was situated in the middle of a bedroom wall: the occupant was using it to store women's shoes; and later, in the chic and stately Dakota, the walls of an apartment the couple had inspected were completely covered over by massive paintings of nude men and women looking earnest and absorbed while engaged in injecting themselves with drugs.

"Oh, well, they could be diabetics," the wife had noted kindly.

"You smell real good."

Freeboard turned a dead gaze to the elevator operator. He was eyeing her with grudging surmise. "Peach bubble bath," Freeboard told him inscrutably. The scent wafted up from her neck.

"Nice earrings," the operator nodded.

"Thanks."

"Hey, Eddie, come *on,* fer chrissakes! *Hold up!*"

An irritated workman was pounding on a door as the elevator creakily lurched up past him.

The diminutive operator called down loudly, "You guys all smell like crap! You stink! I got real nice people with me here!"

The workman's voice rumbled up in a guttural threat:

"You're gonna pay for this, Eddie, you fuck!"

The couple from Hinsdale liked the apartment. Then something extraordinary occurred: standing at a window and breathing in plaster dust as she absently stared at a motor launch plowing white furrows in the murk of the river, Joan Freeboard, relentless pursuer of escrows, indomitable realtor of the Year many times, whirled around to the couple and asked impulsively, "Are you sure you want to live in the city? It's mean and it's dirty and crowded and ugly."

What the hell am I saying? thought the realtor, aghast.

She glanced at the launch again. Something about it. What? She wrinkled her brow. She didn't know. She turned back to the couple and struggled to recover:

"How about a contemporary in Greenwich?"

The strangeness pursued her. Later in the day, the deal done, papers signed, Freeboard found herself walking to Manhattan's last Automat, where she sat at a speckled-beige table with a heaping plate of steaming white rice and baked beans, stirred and mixed them together and ate them ravenously. For her drink she'd taken wedges of lemon that were meant for iced tea from an open bin, squeezed the juice into a glass filled with ice and cold water and now added sugar from a shaker on the table, just as she had done in her impoverished teens. The rice and beans filled her warmly now. Had they not she might have filled an empty bowl with hot water, added salt and gobs of catsup from the bottle on her table, then stirred it to smoothness: tomato soup. Why am I doing this? she wondered. She looked over at the banks of small-windowed compartments of food that would unlock when fed coins through a slot. She was searching for the hot apple pie with rum sauce. Once a March wind had blown a dollar to her chest and that was the day she'd been able to afford it. Where was it? Perhaps she had room for one bite.

"You come here often?"

Freeboard shifted her glance to the homeless bum now seated across from her like a curse. His greasy gray hair flowed down to his shoulders and he wore an old oversized army overcoat, a soiled denim shirt and khaki pants.

"Ya look like an actress. Ever done any actin'? I'm a castin' agent," the bum asserted.

He smelled of stale wine and the air of packing crates and of doorways and steamy grates. A big toe poked up through a hole in his sneaker. The nail needed clipping.

"Also a producer," he added urbanely.

"Yeah, right, you remind me of David O. Selznick."

"Remind? Who the hell ya think you're talkin' to, kiddo? Show a little respect here, okay? Show some class. I see ya ain't got no money for food. I could help you."

"You look like you could use a little help yourself."

Something stirred in the old bum's eyes, some buried recollection of another life. He leaned in to Freeboard, his jaw jutting forward. "It ain't over," he defied her, "till the fat lady sings."

Stifling a smile of rue and compassion, the realtor looked down into her blue leather purse, plucked out something from her wallet and slid it across the beige table to the bum.

"I think you must have dropped this, Mr. O. Selznick."

It was a one-hundred-dollar bill.

"A C-note!"

Freeboard stood up and turned to leave.

"Just a second," said the bum.

The realtor looked back at him.

"I charge *two* hundred dollars for interviews."

Freeboard nodded, appraising him fondly, as if she had met a kindred spirit. An image of her alcoholic father flashed to mind, harshly slapping at her six-year-old's face until it purpled. *"You gonna do what I tell you now, bitch?" "No!"* "Attaway, old champ," approved the realtor. "Go get 'em. Don't ever let the bastards get you down, keep on fighting." Then she turned and prided out into the jostling street where the rumble of trucks, the gasp of buses braking, and the strident honking of horns and the dreams, the hurts, the spites, the fears, the schemes of the hellbent crush of pedestrians rushing for their trains hit her psyche like a wave that washed away from her mind all clouds, all webs, all thoughts that had nattered at its edge, unfocused, and recharged her with the energy that made her Joan Freeboard, child-woman on the make, do or die.

Do or die.

That night in her penthouse on Central Park West, the only sound was the scuffing of soft leather slippers over wide-planked polished oaken floors as the realtor, in a belted forest-green bathrobe, pensively wandered from room to room mulling over a curious proposition that had walked her way a few days before:

"DID I HEAR YOU *say* twenty *percent?*"

"*You did.*"

"*What's the catch?*"

"*My clients want the best. That's you.*"

"*But you told me nothing's happened there for years.*"

"*Nothing has.*"

"*So then put it on a multiple and lower the price. What's the problem?*"

"*The problem is the house's reputation. Dark memories die slowly, Mrs. Freeboard.*"

"*Miss.*"

"*Miss. Think it over, would you please?*"

"*Yeah, I will.*"

FREEBOARD DRIFTED TO a small, round, white-pine table in the corner of her cherrywood-paneled study. On the table was a map, some printed sheets, a brochure, and several photos of a massive mansion crouched upon an island in the Hudson River. Freeboard slipped her hand into a pocket of her robe, withdrew a lighter and a package of Camel Lites. She lit one, dragged deeply, and picked up a photo, then she exhaled smoke and shook her head. No way, it's a waste of time, she lamented; this screwed-up house is straight out of *Dark Shadows*. Brooding and oblong, made of gray stone, it was gabled and crenelated like an old Scottish castle, like Glamis, and here and there a sinister conical tower rose up like an eruption of evil thought. Freeboard sighed and let the photo flutter back to the table, where it landed with a soft, thin, papery click. Too bad this piece of shit's not in Greenwich, she dismally mused; I could sell it for a fortune in a week. Yet she lingered by the table, picking at the photos, tantalized, drawn by this challenge to her boredom. Only You, Dick Daring, she reflected; right? At the edge of her consciousness she heard the crackle of her answering machine, her recorded announcement, a pause and then a hangup. Harry, she thought. She shook her head. Then her glance shifted over to a black leather folder containing the history of the house. She'd only skimmed it; since her youth she'd been afflicted with a mild dyslexia, a gift of brutal beatings by her alcoholic father, undernourishment, and long and frequent absences from school. Reading was arduous for her, a defeat. An assistant handled writing up most of her contracts. All she knew about the house was what she'd been told: that it was built in 1937 by a doctor who murdered his wife in some horrible fashion and immediately afterwards killed himself.

She picked up the folder. On the cover in large white letters was a word that she could read without strain: "ELSEWHERE." And abruptly she remembered a fragment of her dream: a strange place. Some peril. Someone trying to save her, some luminous being, like an angel, like Clarence in It's a Wonderful Life. In the dream he had told her his name, something memorable; now she strained to recall it but couldn't.

The phone and then the click of the answering machine. She tilted her head to the side a bit, listening. Not Harry: Elle Redmund, the wife of James Redmund, celebrated publisher of Vanities Magazine: "...awfully cheeky of me, really, but this friend of ours has popped into town for the night, and we'd both rather die or go to France with Club Med than miss out on your fabulous party. Would you mind if we...?"

Freeboard dropped the folder to the table, stubbed out her cigarette, lit another, then returned to her brow-creasing, thoughtful pacing, randomly scuffing from room to room like a chain-smoking wraith condemned to this vigil in a well-appointed, rent-controlled corridor of hell. About her were no photographs, no traces of a personal history, of affection or of unhappy times; but now and then she would pause in front of a painting, a small Monet or a Picasso miniature, not admiring its beauty or its craft but only taking wan comfort in the knowledge of its cost. Then again she would wander and puff and think until at last she grew weary and fell into her downy-soft four-poster bed, where she lay staring up at her mirrored ceiling groping for a way to solve the puzzle of the house. Once she heard an elevator cage clatter open, then a front door key slipping into the lock; Antonia and George, her live-in help, coming back from an evening off. She sighed and turned over. It's a bitch but you can whip it, she brooded. *Think!* She soon fell asleep. And dreamed of her father, drunk and naked, chasing her high school date down the street. Then she dreamed of the angel again. He was winged and tall and magnificent, but his face was an ovoid blank. In the dream she was waiting for a table at the Palm, a narrow little steak house on Manhattan's East Side, and the angel was attentively taking an order from a young and beautiful dark-eyed woman when abruptly he looked up and met Freeboard's gaze and warned, "Take the train. The clams aren't safe." "What the hell is your name?" the puzzled realtor had shouted at him then and at that she was suddenly awake. She groaned and peered over at her digital clock. It was 6 a.m. *Forget it. Too early.* She lay back and stared up at the mirrored ceiling. "The clams aren't safe?" she puzzled. What was *that?* Moments later her thoughts curled back to the mansion. The agent in charge of the owners' affairs had explained how she could see it at any time. She abruptly sat up. Today would be the day.

COMFORTABLE IN JEANS, western boots and white sweater, Freeboard drove her green Mercedes Cabriolet with the top down across the George Washington Bridge and then north along the Hudson to Craven's Cove, a tiny and sparsely populated village, and from there she took a motor launch across to the island. At the wheel of the boat was its sole crew and owner, a taciturn, slender man in his sixties with brine-wrinkled skin and squinting eyes that were the pale bluish gray of a faded seashell. As they chugged through the mists of the morning river, he squinted at the mansion and asked "You gonna live there?" Freeboard couldn't hear him. There was wind and the engine's whiskey growl. She cupped a hand to her ear, raised her voice, and asked, "*What?*"

"I said, you gonna *live* there?"

For a moment she stared into those faded denim eyes, then glanced up at the stitching on the old salt's nautical cap and the name of the boat: FAR TRAVELER. She turned back to the mansion.

"No."

When they docked, the old ferryman remained on the launch, lighting up a briar pipe while he leaned against a rail and watched Freeboard as she clumped down the dock's old planks and then entered a shadowy grove of great oaks until at last he couldn't see her anymore. She troubled him. He didn't know why.

The realtor followed a gravel path that snaked through the wood about a tenth of mile and led her directly to the front of the house. Beside the front door she found a realtor's lockbox, expertly twiddled the combination, extracted a key, and then turned for a look at her wider surroundings. Past the woods she caught a glimpse of a shoreline and beach next to waters breathing placid and shallow and clear, and beyond, in a shimmer of sun and haze, gleamed the jutting and sprawling skyline of Manhattan, looming tall and commanding and implacably unhaunted.

She peered up at the mansion's forbidding hulk. *Very good,* she thought, satisfied. *It's not staring back. So far the fucking house has done nothing wrong.*

The river's breath caught a bright green scent from the trees, smelling sweet, and the earth and sky were quiet. Freeboard heard the soft rippling sound of her key slipping over the metal serrations of the door lock. She turned, pushed inward and entered the house.

She was standing in a gracious, vaulted entry hall. Beyond a pair of oak doors that stood open, she beheld a huge Great Room ghostly with furnishings bulging and misshapen under white slipcovers meant to guard them from dust and the beat of the sun. The owner—the heir to the original builder—and his family, a wife and two very young children, had been living in Florence for the past three years, and the house, though available for sale or lease, had during that time remained untenanted. No one would buy it or live there. "Haunted."

With a lazy gait, lips puckered judiciously, Freeboard ambled into the room and then stopped with her hands on her hips and looked around. The room's high ceiling was heavily beamed in the crisscross style of an old Spanish mission, and in the middle of a wall a huge firepit yawned. The realtor

moved forward, her boot heels thudding on the random-width planks of a hickory floor as she prowled through the room pulling covers off the furnishings, and when she'd finished she found herself surprised: filled with groupings of overstuffed sofas and chairs that were upholstered in homey and reassuring paisleys, the room was a warm invitation to life that included a game table, stereo equipment, and an eight-foot Steinway, gleaming and inviting, as down upon all, from the high gabled windows, shafted columns of relentlessly cheerful sunlight. *So where's Christopher Lee and the freaking Fangettes?* Freeboard glanced to her left and a cozy bar in a fireplaced library bristling with books, and then sauntered past a wide and curving staircase that led up to several bedrooms off a second-floor hall. Then she paused as she noticed that there was an alcove tucked like a secret under the stairs. She walked over and discovered there, lost in shadow, an arched ornamental oaken door that had carved into its center, like an ugly threat, an icily unsettling gargoylish face whose mouth gaped open in a taut and malevolent grin and with eyes bulging wide with rage.

Freeboard stared back and uttered quietly, "Asshole."

She gripped the brass doorknob and attempted to open the door but discovered that she couldn't. It was locked.

Ping.

A faint sound tinged the silence behind her, something like the muted single note of a piano. She turned around slowly and stared at the Steinway, half expecting to see someone sitting at the keys. There were several other wings to the house, she'd been told, including quarters and a separate kitchen for staff. There might have been a caretaker somewhere about. But there was no one there, she saw. She was alone. She walked to the piano and lifted the keyboard cover, and then, leaning over with a grin, began to play "Put on a Happy Face" as she looked all around and then called out loudly, "This is for you, you crazy house!"

Then she stopped and stared pensively.

"But what do we do to make someone come and see you?"

The house did not answer.

Fine. Be that way.

SHE DROVE BACK to Manhattan lost in ponder, gave the car to her doorman, rode up to her apartment, let herself in and went straight to her study, where she sat and began to tug off her boots.

"Evening, Madam."

Antonia, the maid, had come in.

"You are going out for dinner, Missus?"

"No. I'll eat at seven."

"Very good."

"Tell George to fix me a Cajun martini, would you, Tony?"

"Yes, Missus. Something else?"

Freeboard finished tugging off a boot, dropped it, and then scrutinized the housekeeper carefully, frowning. "You look tired. You've got bags. Are you sleeping okay?"

"Not so good."

"Are you worried about something?"

"No, Missus."

"You sure, Tony?"

"Yes. I am sure."

"I think maybe you're working too hard."

The housekeeper diffidently shrugged and looked away.

"You and George take the day off tomorrow, Antonia."

"Oh, no, Missus!"

"*Yes,* Missus. You do what I say. And you know, I don't feel like much dinner. Just a sandwich. Okay? Just whatever. And would you make that martini a double?"

"Very good, Missus. Yes. Right away."

Dainty in her blue-and-white housemaid's uniform, the middle-aged housekeeper padded away. Freeboard stared at her back with concern. She finished pulling off the other boot, let it drop to the floor, then stretched her legs out and wriggled her toes.

My God, does that feel good!

Staring softly into nothingness, she thought of the mansion again. And then stopped. *Yeah, let's give it a rest.* She leaned her head back on the chair and closed her eyes. Then heard the click of the answering machine coming on. The publisher's wife again, Elle Redmund. "Hello, darling, did you get my other message? Well, never mind; it turns out that our visitor isn't coming after all. Thanks anyway, Joanie. We'll see you Friday night."

Another click.

For a time there was silence and shallow breathing. And then suddenly Freeboard's eyes opened wide as, in one of those mysterious events of the spirit wherein the unconscious broods upon data, draws conclusions, then presents them to the mind as inspiration, she experienced a sudden, overwhelming revelation.

There it was! That was it! She knew how to sell the house!

"Your martini, Missus Freeboard."

"Thanks, Tony. Tell George it looks perfect."

"Yes, Missus."

Freeboard took the glass but did not drink. She was plotting.

Not every epiphany originates in grace.

FREEBOARD'S PARTY THAT Friday was lively and crowded, crammed with playwrights, politicians and corporate executives, models and socialites and Mafiosi, anyone who'd ever bought a property from her. For the space of half an hour the hostess was nowhere to be found, nor was her publisher guest, James Redmund. When Freeboard reappeared among her guests, she seemed pleased.

Step One of her plan had been completed.

ON THE FOLLOWING Thursday, five days later, the renowned British psychic, Anna Trawley, sat by a fire while she sipped at tea in the den of her Cotswold cottage in England when a message arrived from a total stranger, an American realtor named Joan Freeboard. Her little face a cameo, delicate and pale, Trawley, in her forties, had a quiet beauty and her small and limpid chestnut eyes glowed faintly with some distant but ineffable sadness on which they seemed constantly inward turned. Beside her on a small, square teakwood table waited mail and a fresh-smelling copy of the *Times,* and on a paneled wall hung a few remembrances: a photo of herself with the Queen; a newspaper headline NOTED PSYCHIC FINDS KILLER; and a photo of a child, a pretty, dimpled young girl who, in the blur of retouching and tinting over the black-and-white photo with pastel colors, seemed lost in some other dimension of time. Beneath an open window lay a plastic Ouija board upon a table with two facing chairs.

"Mum?"

Trawley turned to the girl who had entered, her pretty, young maid, newly hired. "Peta?"

She was holding out a small, round silver tray. Trawley absently stared at a deep white scar tucked into the maid's right eyebrow for a moment, wondering what painful event it commemorated and whether it had happened by chance; then she lowered her gaze to the offered tray. Upon it, in a square dull yellow envelope, lay a cablegram and a message that, by a path at once straight yet labyrinthine—depending on the viewer, man or God—would bond Trawley's destiny forever to Freeboard's.

"Thank you, Peta."

"Yes, mum."

The maid quietly walked out. Trawley picked up the envelope, slipped out its contents and saw that the cable ran on for six pages. She read them and then rested the papers in her lap, put her head back on the chair and closed her eyes. A sudden breeze sprang up from the wooded outdoors that ruffled the white lace curtains of the window, and below them, perhaps pushed by the brief, sharp gust, the coned glass planchette that had rested on the Ouija board slid from the center of the board to the top, and there it rested directly on a word.

The word was *no*.

CHAPTER TWO

I'VE BEEN DEAD FOR eight months, just in case you hadn't noticed." Tall and Byronic, urbane, aristocratic, Terence Dare swabbed his brush at a yellow on the palette and then dabbed at the canvas propped before him in the sunlit, high-ceilinged, pitched-roof studio of his Fire Island home. "Ever since Robert walked out of my life," he mourned in a rich and cultivated voice. "No, I can't write a word," he sighed. "I've no heart."

"Shit shit shit!" muttered Freeboard. "*Shit!*"

Dare wiped a spatter of red from his finger onto the painter's smock that he wore above a T-shirt and faded black denim jeans and then shifted a hooded blue gaze to the realtor, who was smoking and pacing back and forth in agitation, the echoing clacks of her spike-heeled shoes on the oaken floor bouncing up to a skylight. She swatted at a haze of grayish smoke in her path.

"It's the cover of *Vanities,* Terry! The *cover!*"

"Let me get this straight," said the world-famous author: "James Redmund repels you, he's a prig and a bore and is also among that elite corps of rectums who are constantly telling us how much they love a challenge, as if living on a spinning rock hurtling through the void dodging asteroids and comets weren't challenge enough, not to mention tornadoes, death and disease as well as Vlad the Impaler and earthquakes and war, but you laid him anyway?"

"I told you, it was business."

"Are you shtupping for the Mafia now, my precious, and no longer, as usual, for all of mankind?"

"Oh, fuck you, Terry."

"Darling, thousands have tried; only hundreds have succeeded."

Looking chic in her navy Armani suit, the realtor stopped pacing and coughed into her fist. "Gotta quit," she resolved, her eyes smarting and teary. She clattered to a table where she stubbed out her cigarette in a large white seashell ashtray. "Look, I told you, they don't run this kind of stuff. Not normally."

"No, not normally," Dare said inscrutably.

"He's the publisher; he does what he wants."

She kept crushing and tamping the burnt-out butt.

"When and where did you commit this unspeakable act?"

Freeboard flopped down into a chair by a window, crossed her arms and stared sulkily at the author. "Jesus, Terry, you could write it in a week."

"When and where?" Dare persisted.

"At the dinner party Friday. In my bathroom."

"In your *bathroom?*"

She gave a little shrug.

"It's okay. We ran the water real loud."

The author appraised her as if he were measuring the distance to a star. In her small green eyes set close together he could find no trace of blush or guile; their expression was just as he had always observed it to be, which was blank and vaguely expectant. It was as if she were eternally awaiting further comment. Her soul is a wide-open window, he reflected; she's as simple and direct as a shopping cart.

"You could write the fucking thing in an *hour*."

And more tenacious than the grip of a deep tattoo.

"Now let's see if this is right..." Dare started expressionlessly.

She looked away and rolled her eyes. "You always do this."

"You've been offered the exclusive listing on Elsewhere," he reviewed, "but the problem, it would seem, is that it's haunted and—"

"It's no such thing! Nothing's happened there in years! I mean it's just that it's got this shitty-creepy reputation."

The winner of a Pulitzer Prize for Literature stared numbly.

"Shitty-creepy?"

"So okay, I'm not a writer."

"You're a criminal. You've lined up Anna Trawley, the world-famous psychic; the renowned Dr. Gabriel Case of NYU, *the* authority in all such matters, smile-smirk; the four of us then spend a few nights in the house, and while Trawley and Case take baths in the vibes and discover nothing ghostly or unusual whatever, I observe, making copious notes, of course, and then I write a little shitty-witty article about it that thoroughly debunks the idea that it's haunted; your pipe-smoking bathroom incubus prints it, the house's reputation is now Caesar's wife and you sell it and get filthier rich than ever. Does that sum it up fairly, my Angel of the Closings?"

"I've been offered a triple commission on this, Terry. That's seven fucking figures."

"Must we really use the eff word so incessantly?"

"We must!"

"Then might we please pronounce it 'fyook' or something, precious? I mean, really."

Aloofly, he turned and examined the painting, a swirling melange of varied shades of vivid yellow. Freeboard leaped up from her chair and approached him. "You owe me, Terry!"

Dare lifted his brush to paint.

"Now it comes, the deadly rocket attack on my guilt."

"You're *denying* that you owe me?"

"Sigmund Freud would have killed for your gifts."

She planted herself in front of him and folded her arms across her chest. "You're *denying* it?"

He looked down at his bright red Nike tennis shoes and then shook his head and sighed. "No, I owe you," he admitted. "I owe you immensely. You've always been there for me on the Dawn Patrol, all those endless, awful nights when I needed a shoulder that I knew wasn't padded with secret envies and lies and spites." His eye caught a glistening blue on his palette. "You're steadfast and loyal and completely unexpected, my Joan; you're the only living human that I trust. Still, I'll have to disappoint you on this, I'm afraid."

"For godssakes, it's just a magazine article, Terry! You could have a broken heart and still write a freaking *article,* couldn't you!"

He looked up at her with quiet incredulity.

"I mean, it's not like a book or something!"

"No, it's not like a book," he said tonelessly.

"What's that look for?"

"What look?"

"*That* look."

"I am probing for the source of your feral cunning."

"Meaning what? What does *feral* mean?"

"Anything relating to the national government."

Glaring, he turned back to the canvas and painted.

"Oh, was that some kind of faggoty joke?"

"As you like it."

"Come on, Terry, quit kidding around and do the piece."

"I would love to but it's simply not possible."

"Even though this freaking deal means the world to me?"

"Yes."

"And all because of some weight-lifting wannabe model you picked up in the park feeding steroids to the pigeons? I'm not getting this, Terry; I'm not getting this at all."

"My dear Joanie, there is more to this matter than Robert," sighed the author. Freeboard watched him intently, frowning; there was something evasive in his manner and his voice. "In fact, there's a *great* deal more," Dare asserted.

"Yeah, like what?"

"Well, just more."

"What more? Come on, what? Be specific."

"It's just writing itself."

"What about it?"

"I've given it up forever."

Freeboard clutched at her forehead and cried out, *"Fyook!"*

"It's too hard, love," Dare told her, "too many decisions. 'Had a wonderful day,' it says in Oscar Wilde's diary: 'I inserted a comma, removed it, then decided to reinsert it.' Joanie, writing is dross."

"I'm not believing this, Terry!"

"It is mental manual labor. As of now, I consider myself a painter."

Freeboard's frustrated glance darted over to the canvas, swiftly taking in its spiraling yellow meanderings. Her eyes narrowed in dismal surmise.

"What the hell is this supposed to be, Terry?"

"*Lemons Resting.*"

She reached out and grabbed the brush from his hand, looking worried. "Are you dropping LSD again, Terry?"

"Oh, don't be so silly," Dare sniffed.

"No more camels in cheap orange taffeta dresses who swear they're Jehovah's Witnesses sneaking in the house at night to talk about your books?"

"You haven't even a shred of common decency, have you?"

"No, I don't."

"And all of this because I've given up writing?"

"Yeah, yeah, yeah: first it's Robert and a broken heart and then writing is a pain in the ass and you're Picasso. This is sounding like bullshit to me, Terry. Are you scared? You believe in stupid ghosts, for chrissakes?"

"That's absurd!"

Dare's cheeks glowed pink. He recovered the brush and turned back to his canvas. "Look, the fact of the matter, if you really want to know, is that I simply couldn't bear to go away and leave the dogs."

"Now I *know* this is bullshit."

"It isn't," Dare insisted.

"You'd ruin my life for those two little fucks?"

Dare turned and glared down at her stonily. "Am I to presume that by 'those two little fucks' you are referring to those sweetest, most refined toy poodles, Pompette and Maria-Hidalgo LaBlanche?"

Freeboard glared back, her face inches from his chest.

"So bring them with us."

"I beg your pardon?"

"Bring them with us. Bring the dogs."

"Bring the dogs?"

Something faintly like panic edged his voice.

"Yeah, we'll bring 'em."

"No, it simply wouldn't work."

"It wouldn't work?"

"No, it wouldn't."

"Why not?" Freeboard asked him.

"I don't know."

"You don't know? You're scared shitless, you literary asshole! Do you sleep with a nightlight, you flaming fyook?"

"*Fyook* has never been a noun," Dare said coldly.

"It is now," shot back Freeboard.

"Poor usage. Furthermore, your vile and repellent accusations, Miss Whoever You Are, are absurd if not pathetic."

"Are they true?"

The author flushed.

"Why don't you find some other writer, for heaven's sakes!" he whined. "My God, Joanie, *Vanities* can get you your pick!"

"Well, they picked."

"'They picked'? What on earth do you mean?"

THEY WERE SITTING AT *a window table for two in the Hotel Sherry Netherland bar. It was not quite five o'clock and the tables on either side were still empty. "Hold it," said Freeboard. She was groping through a briefcase. "There's a really spooky picture of the house. Let me find it." Troubled and distracted, the publisher* of Vanities *darted an apprehensive glance at the door as he heard another patron coming in from the street. It was no one that he knew, he saw with relief. Nervously tapping the stem of an unlit briar pipe against his teeth, he shifted his fretful gaze back to Freeboard. "Four of us alone in a haunted house," she effused, "and Terry's first magazine piece ever!"*

A waiter placed a chilled Manhattan cocktail softly on the crisp white tablecloth in front of her, and then a glass of chardonnay in front of Redmund. "Chardonnay, sir?"

"Right," murmured Redmund. "Thanks." In his eyes, open wide and faintly bulging, an incipient hysteria quietly lurked. When the waiter had gone he leaned his head in to Freeboard. "Don't you think we should talk about what happened at the party?"

"Oh, what happened?" Freeboard absently responded, still groping through her purse for the photos. And then abruptly looked up with a stunned realization. "Oh, what happened!" Her hands flew to Redmund's, squeezing them ardently. "Oh, yes, Jim! That's all I want to talk about, think about! Come on, let's get this article out of the way and then we can get back to real life, to us! Do you like it? You'll publish it?"

"It's interesting, Joan," observed Redmund.

Freeboard let go of his hands, leaned back, and then folded her arms and looked away.

"Yeah, right."

She knew very well what "interesting" meant.

"But it really isn't right for us," Redmund pleaded. "Joan, look...The other night was incredible."

"Sure."

"Just amazing. More exciting than anything I think I've ever known."

"Yeah, me too," Freeboard murmured. She was dully staring at the decorative fountain directly across from the Plaza Hotel.

"But it was wrong, love, we made a mistake," Redmund faltered. "I thought it all over today while I was jogging and..."

Freeboard turned to stare at him in blank surmise.

"Well, I could never leave my wife," said the publisher firmly. "I just couldn't. This is taking us nowhere, Joanie. If I didn't tell you now there'd be a lot more pain down the line. I'm sorry. I'm so terribly sorry."

The realtor continued to stare at him numbly, her eyes growing wider in disbelief.

"You're sorry," she echoed.

He gloomed into his drink.

"Yes, I know; that's a lame word, isn't it—sorry."

Redmund heard a single, stifled sob, looked up and saw Freeboard choking back tears. "Ah, dammit," he fumbled. The realtor clutched at her linen napkin and held it tightly to her face; she appeared to be weeping into it softly.

"I feel awful...horrible," Redmund groped. "Now how do I live in that condo you sold me? I'll be seeing you everywhere... in every hallway, every square of parquet."

This seemed to propel the weeping real estate broker to a noticeably higher emotional pitch, although one could not confidently distinguish, with anything approaching absolute certitude, her sudden, soft moan of pain from a desperate attempt to stifle a guffaw. Redmund glanced around to see if anyone was watching them, and then fumbled at emptying his pipe. "Listen, Joanie, that article; it sounds—well, very challenging. Really. You're certain that Terence would do it?"

"REDMUND WON'T DO it unless you write it," said Freeboard, concluding her account of the meeting.

"You are Liza Doolittle's evil twin."

"Liza Who?"

Dare assessed the avid shine in her eyes, the lower lip jutting out, the dimpled chin tilted upward defiantly. He saw the frightened child inside. "It isn't the money at all, is it Joanie? It's that ravenous tiger burning bright in your soul, that desperate drive to stay ahead, to keep winning, that need to keep proving that you're really okay."

She frowned and looked puzzled. "It isn't the money?"

Abruptly a door from the beach clicked open and into the room bounded two yapping poodles, their claws etching clittering sounds on the floor. They were followed by a clubfooted man in his forties, a houseman Dare had hired years before out of pity.

Freeboard glared at a poodle that had stopped at her feet and was staring at her leg with intense speculation. "Don't even *think* about it," she threatened, "or I'm turning you into a tiny rug."

"Go, Maria! Scoot!" Dare warned. "She's a killer! Run! She meant it!" He looked over at the houseman. "Pierre, *sortez les chiens.*"

The houseman nodded and replied. *"Immdiatemont."* He clapped his hands at the dogs. *"Allez les chiens! Allez sortez! Nous allons dehors!"* The dogs skittered away through an inner door and the houseman followed them, one shoulder low, a shoe clumping.

"This means a whole lot to me, Terry. A lot."

The author turned his leonine head to her and stared. He had bought this very house through Freeboard's offices, it was how he had come to meet her; yet never since that time had she asked him for anything, not even for a copy of one of his books. His celebrity meant nothing to the girl, that he knew; and that, for some reason, she cared for him deeply. He searched her eyes for the secret wounds that he'd learned to detect behind their gleam of self-will.

"A *whole* lot," she repeated.

"And how long would we be there?"

"Five days."

She explained how Dr. Gabriel Case, the psychologist, professor and expert on the subject of hauntings, would precede them to the house with his special equipment and set it all up before they arrived.

Most of their luggage would be sent on ahead, and when Anna Trawley had landed in New York they would all take a limo to Craven's Cove, where the motor launch would carry them across to the island. "Case is making all the arrangements," she finished. "I mean like the phones and utilities and crud."

"How very sporting."

"Yeah, he's neat."

"He's *neat?*"

"Oh, well, at least on the phone. I've never met him."

"You conned him into doing all of this on the *phone?*"

"Come on, Terry, I'm paying him a bundle. Okay?"

"Oh, I see." The author turned stiffly to his painting. "So the fix is in. I should have known."

The realtor frowned and moved in closer.

"Listen, let's get serious," she said.

"Oh, yes, serious."

"Margoittai is packing all our meals. The whole time we're at the house we'll be eating Four Seasons."

The author's brush stroke froze in midair.

"'Ah, Mephistopheles!'"

"Is that a yes?"

The year was 1993.

Later on there would be serious doubts about that.

PART TWO

CHAPTER THREE

THE CARVED FRONT door of the mansion burst open as if by the force of a desperate thought. "Holy shit, is this a hurricane or what!" exclaimed Freeboard. Sopping in a glistening yellow sou'wester provided by the captain of the launch *Far Traveler*, she staggered and tumbled into the entry hall with a keening wind at her back. She turned to see Dare rushing up the front stoop, and Trawley, carrying a bag, behind him, slower, deliberate and unhurried. A rain of all the waters of the earth pelted down.

Freeboard cupped a hand to her mouth: "You okay, Mrs. Trawley?" she squalled.

"Oh, yes, dear!" the psychic called back. "I'm fine!"

A booming thunder gripped the sky by the shoulders and shook it. The sudden storm that had arisen as they crossed had been a terror, buffeting the launch with tempestuous waves. Hurricane warnings had been issued that morning, but the winds had been expected to diminish at landfall. This had not occurred.

Dare entered and dropped a light bag to the floor. "Joan, I owe you a flogging for this," he vowed. "I knew that I never should have done it."

"Well, you did it," Freeboard told him. "Now for shitssakes, watch your mouth around these people, would you, Terry? I had to practically beg them to do this."

"Thank heaven I gave you no trouble."

Freeboard lifted off her windjammer hat, and then gestured to the open door, where the psychic seemed to falter as she climbed the front steps. "Terry, give Mrs. Trawley a hand."

"Oh, very well."

Dare giraffed toward the psychic with a limp, loose gait and reached out for her bag. "May I help you?"

"Oh, no thank you. I'm fine. I travel light."

"Yes, of course. Tambourines weigh almost nothing."

"*Jesus*, Terry!"

Trawley entered, swept her hat off and set down her bag. "That's all right," she told Freeboard benignly; "I didn't hear it." In fact, she had heard enough from Dare in the limo, including a request to compare her methods with those of Whoopi Goldberg in the motion picture *Ghost,* in addition to a penetrating follow-up question concerning the cholesterol content of ectoplasm. At each sally, Trawley nodded her head and smiled faintly, mutely staring out serenely at the landscape through her window, and the effect of this on Dare had at last begun to show: with every mile that brought him closer to the island and the mansion, his darts at matters psychic or supernatural had grown increasingly frequent and acerbic. "Edgar Cayce reportedly first went into trance," he asserted as the limousine neared Bear Mountain, "as an excuse for not going to school, and when someone claimed a frog that he had kept in his pocket was somehow cured of mononucleosis, why, of course, people tended to sit up and take notice."

Freeboard leaned into the wind and shut the door. In the silence, it was Dare who first noticed the music. "Dearest God, am I in heaven?" he exclaimed. "Cole Porter!" The author's face was aglow with a child's first joy as from behind the stout doors that led into the Great Room drifted a melody played on a piano.

Dare beamed. "My favorite: 'Night and Day'!"

Freeboard moved toward the doors.

"That you in there, Doc?" she called out.

"Miss Freeboard?"

The voice from within was deep and pleasant and oddly unmuffled by the thickness of the doors. Freeboard opened them wide and stepped into the Great Room. All of its lamps were lit and glowing, splashing the wood-paneled walls with life, and in the crackle of the firepit flames leapt cheerily, blithe to the longing in the notes of "Night and Day." Freeboard breathed in the scent of burning pine from the fire. The howlings of the storm were a world away.

"Yeah, we're here!" she called out to the man at the piano. She smiled, moving toward him, while at the same time removing her dripping sou'wester. Behind her strode Dare and, more slowly, Anna Trawley. Freeboard's boots made a squishing sound. They were soaked.

"Ah, yes, there you all are again, safe and sound," said the man at the piano. "I'm so glad. I was worried."

He had strong good looks, Freeboard noticed: long wavy black hair above a chiseled face that seemed torn whole from some mythic quarry. The firelight flickered and danced in his eyes and she saw that they were dark but wasn't sure of their color. She judged him in his forties or perhaps early fifties. He was wearing a short-sleeved khaki shirt and khaki pants.

"This storm is amazing, don't you think?" he exclaimed. "Did you order this weather, Mr. Dare? Are you to blame?"

Dare was noted for his Gothic mystery novels.

"I believe I ordered Chivas," the author said crisply. He and Freeboard had arrived at the piano and stopped while Anna Trawley hung back beside a grouping of furniture that was clustered around the fireplace. She was glancing all around the room with a puzzled and uncertain, tentative air.

"Are you a ghost?"

Dare was speaking to the man at the piano.

Freeboard turned to him, incredulous.

"What crap is this?" she hissed in an irritated undertone.

"That's how they show them on the spook ride at Disneyland," said Dare in a full, firm voice: "A lot of spirits dancing while a big one plays piano."

"I'll strangle your dogs, you little creep!" Freeboard gritted.

Anna Trawley sank down into an overstuffed chair and fixedly stared at the man at the piano. "I'm Gabriel Case," he declared. He stood up. "I'm quite honored that you've come, Mr. Dare. And Mrs. Trawley."

"Oh, please don't stop playing!" Dare insisted.

"Then I won't."

Case sat down and began to play "All Through the Night." Freeboard stood quietly studying him. His eyes, she now saw, were pitch-black, so that even his casual gaze seemed to pierce, and down from his cheekbone almost to his jaw raced a vivid, deep scar that jagged like lightning. Freeboard heard a muted roll of thunder far away; the rain on the windows was patting more softly now, like a melancholy background for the song.

"So, Miss Freeboard," Case continued. His smile now was brilliant. Like a fucking archangel, the realtor thought. "I'm so glad to meet the face behind the telephone at last," Case said. "And a lovely face at that, if I may say so."

"How long have you been here?" Freeboard asked.

"Seems forever. What's the matter, Miss Freeboard? You're frowning."

"You don't look like your picture," she said. She moved closer, appraising him intently, looking puzzled. She added, "The one on the back of the book."

"*Ghosts and Hauntings?*"

Freeboard nodded.

"Yes, they wanted something spooky," he told her, "so they posed me in a very strange light."

"Guess they did."

"I've read all of your works, Mr. Dare," Case effused. "All quite wonderful. Really."

"Thank you."

"My absolute favorite was *Gilroy's Confession.*" Case lifted his hands from the keys of the piano. He was looking at Freeboard. "There you go again," he said, not unpleasantly. "What's wrong?"

For once again she was frowning.

"This has happened before," she said oddly.

Case leaned in to her as if he hadn't heard. "What was that?"

"I'm having *déjà vu*," she answered.

"This is neither the time nor the place," snapped Dare.

Case chuckled and Freeboard was bewildered as to why.

The author glanced up at a painting high on the wall above the massive fireplace, a life-sized figure of a man in the dress of a bygone time, perhaps the thirties. Though the rest of the painting had a sharp and rich presence, the face of its subject was milky and occluded, presenting a hazy, oval blank.

"Who's this?" Dare asked.

Case looked up. "Dr. Edward Quandt, the original owner."

"Why on earth is his face like that?" Dare wondered.

In the shadows Trawley looked up at the painting.

Case nodded. "Yes, it's strange," he observed. "Very strange."

"It's the haircut."

Case turned and saw Freeboard staring at him thoughtfully. "Yeah, I think that's it," she went on. "That's what's different. It's the haircut."

"Hello?"

Warm and mysterious, a field of dark flowers, the husky voice floated across the room with the breath of some indefinable emotion, like remembrance of a long-lost summer or of grace.

Case stared past the others. His expression had changed.

"Ah, here's Morna," he said very softly.

Her head slightly angled to the side, as if questioning, a lissome young woman was

slowly approaching them, moving with a soft and gliding motion like a figure in the corridors of a dream. Her features were rawboned and rugged, imperfect, with protruding high cheekbones and a large jutting jaw, and yet she gave an effect of sensuality and beauty. She wore a paisley-printed purplish taffeta skirt, a white shirt and a silken red string tie. Set deep in the shadowed gold of her skin, her widely spaced pale green eyes were startling. Case stood up slowly and met her gaze.

"Yes," she said, halting before them. "I have come."

Her long black hair cascaded to her shoulders, smelling of hyacinth and morning. For a moment Case continued to stare. "Morna, these are our guests," he said at last. "Miss Freeboard. Mr. Dare."

"How do you do?" said the girl. Her brief glance took them in.

"And Mrs. Trawley," Case added with a gesture toward the psychic. "Mrs. Trawley is clairvoyant, Morna."

The girl turned and fixed her bright green gaze on Trawley. She held it there for seconds. And then she turned back and slightly nodded. "Yes."

"Morna is my housekeeper," Case explained. "No one else lives on the island, as you know; we're quite isolated here. Morna's kindly volunteered to help out."

"Aren't there people in the town across the way?" asked Dare.

A faint, high note of strain tinged his voice.

"Yes, there are," answered Case, "but..."

He hesitated, silently searching their faces.

"But what?" Dare demanded a bit too crisply.

Case took the author's sou'wester from his hands. "Well, you're quite soaked through," he said. "We can talk this all over later on; you know, try to get properly acquainted and all. But for now I'm sure you're anxious to get into dry clothes. Morna, kindly show our friends to their rooms, would you please?"

"Your hair was longer in the picture," said Freeboard. *"That's* the difference." Once again she was fixedly staring at Case.

Case turned to her, smiling a little, and he paused. In his eyes some ambiguous emotion lurked, like a wanly affectionate, patient sadness. He held the realtor's gaze, then spoke quietly. "Yes."

BY LATE THAT MORNING, once again the rain had quickened and Freeboard was pacing back and forth in her room. She had a phone at her ear and kept irritably whipping the cord from her path. Again and again she breathed out, "This is nuts!"

In addition to an attic section and a basement, the mansion's rooms were arranged on three levels. The investigators' rooms were all a-row along a hallway on the second floor overlooking the Great Room. Freeboard's suite was the closest to the staircase. Spacious and airy, it had its own fireplace, a high vaulted ceiling and heavy wood beams, but its only two windows were high and narrow, so that both of the bedside lamps were turned on, pouring light on a green leather Gucci suitcase wide open and half emptied out atop the bed, an ornately carved, quilt-covered wooden four-poster. Freeboard hadn't yet bothered to change her clothes and was still in her stonewashed shirt and jeans. Once arrived in the room she'd thought hotly, *God we're here! We're really doing it! It's actually happening! We're here!* Manically energized and elated, she had only taken time to tug off her wet boots and pull on a dry pair of fluffy white woolen socks. She stopped pacing and wriggled her toes in them now as she listened to the ringing at the end of the line; hypnotically regular and low, it seemed distant, as if it were ringing in some other dimension. Freeboard took the phone from her ear and eyed it, frowning and squinting in consternation. She'd dialed her office and no one had answered. And then she'd redialed again and again. On this try she had counted more than fifty rings. She breathed "Christ!" and then clumped to an antique desk where she slammed the receiver down into its cradle. "It's freaking *impossible*!" she vehemently murmured. Hands on her hips, she stared down at the phone, and for a moment the lamplights flickered and dimmed before surging back up to their former brightness. Freeboard peered around the room, her eyes slits, as she grittily murmured, "Don't try that crap on *me*!"

She heard a sound, a deep rapping from the wall beside the mirror. Expressionless, she shifted her glance to the spot.

Through the wall came the voice of Dare, low and muffled:

"Are you there?"

"No."

"This wall sounds hollow to me."

"No shit."

"Does your room have any windows?"

"What's it to you?"

"I feel smothered. And I keep hearing creaking sounds."

"Stop walking. It's an old wooden floor."

"You have no heart, bitch."

"No."

There came a single loud rap from the other side.

"This wall is *definitely* hollow," worried Dare.

Freeboard curled in her lips. Her eyes narrowed.

"Goddamit, that's *just* what I was afraid of!"

Grimly, the realtor strode out into the hallway and up to the door of the room next to hers, where she grasped the doorknob, threw the door open, walked in and loudly slammed the door shut behind her. "Listen here, Too Little, Too Latent," she began.

Dare flinched. He'd been standing with his ear to a wall, a round stone paperweight lifted in his hand. He was clad in a full-length white mink dressing gown.

Freeboard strode across the room and confronted him.

"Do you remember why we're here?" she demanded.

Dare looked down at her haughtily. "To break and enter?"

"We are here to clear this fyooking house's fyooking reputation!"

Freeboard snatched the heavy paperweight out of Dare's grasp.

"Knock it off with this rapping and shit!" she warned him. "I thought you were a total nonbeliever!"

"So I am. Can't you see that I was teasing you, precious? And of course you took the bait like a well-famished trout."

"Oh, yeah?"

Dare drew himself up imperiously. "Rest your mind," he said. "I *am* doubt." Then he held out his upturned hand and demanded, "Now would you please be so kind as to return my lucky rock?"

Freeboard hefted the weight.

"Where do you want it?"

"I'VE ALREADY SET UP cameras on timers here and there," explained Case as he added more cream to his coffee. "Please don't trip over them," he cautioned with a smile. He was sitting at the end of an oblong table amid the remains of a savory brunch that had included a bacon-and-onion quiche, prawns sautéed in a coconut mustard sauce, varied jams and assorted pastries and breads. Croissant crumbs speckled the white linen tablecloth and no butter knife was unsmeared. At the opposite end of the table sat Dare, with Freeboard at an angle close beside him, while Trawley sat close to Gabriel Case. The psychic had changed into a gauzy turquoise dress and from her hair a scent of jasmine rose. "I've had all the phones turned on and all that," continued Case. "If you'd like to make a note, the number's 914-2121. Awfully easy to remember. In the meantime, as for now there isn't anything for anyone to do except relax and be terribly observant; and, of course, report anything unusual to me."

The drumming of rain on mullioned windows, looking out to a wood, filled a momentary silence. Then Dare cleared his throat and looked at Case. "Have you ever caught a ghost on film?"

"No, I haven't."

"Well, that's honest," the author admitted. He nodded.

Case sipped at his coffee and then set down his cup. It made a faint little pewtery sound against the saucer. "Mr. Dare," he said, "I do hope you won't take offense but I'm finding the mask a little bit of a distraction."

"Then perhaps you have Attention Deficit Disorder."

Dare wore a Phantom of the Opera mask.

Freeboard reached over and ripped it from his face.

"Thank you," Dare quietly told her.

"You're welcome."

Freeboard folded her arms across her chest, looked away and shook her head with an exasperated sigh. From a pocket Dare produced a transistorized tape recorder. He set it before him on the table.

"Dr. Case, do you mind if I record this?"

"No, of course not. Good idea. Go right ahead."

The author slid a switch on the side of the recorder and a tiny red light flashed on. "There we are," Dare announced. "You may fire when ready, Master Gridley."

Case put his arms on the table, leaning forward. "Do you all know the history of the house?" He scanned their faces.

"No, I don't," said Trawley. Her voice was barely audible. All through the brunch she had hardly said a word, except in answer to a question about her trip and then another concerning a case she'd been involved in, the search for a missing child in Surrey. Mainly, she'd been fixedly staring at Case.

"It was—"

"Built by Dr. Quandt," Dare finished over Case, "in the middle of the thirties for his beautiful wife, whom he came to believe was being grossly unfaithful, resulting in his promptly and savagely offing her."

"I see you've done your homework, Mr. Dare."

The author shrugged. "All I know is what Joanie has told me."

"Yes, Quandt was a violent man," Case confirmed.

"I'm not surprised," answered Dare. "I think surgeons have violent natures, that's the reason they go into that line of work: normal people couldn't slice another person into bits and moments later eat a double Big Mac with fries."

"No, I agree."

"It's rude," added Dare.

"So it is. However, Quandt was not a surgeon," said Case.

"He wasn't?"

"No, Quandt was a noted psychiatrist."

The author turned a frimmled, cool look to the realtor.

Freeboard stared back at him defiantly. "*So?*"

"Quandt was also maniacally jealous," Case offered. "Physician heal thyself and all that. She was very much younger and he loved her intensely."

Dare turned back to him. "What was her name?"

"Her name was Riga." Case glanced up at Morna, who had entered from the kitchen and was quietly approaching him with a silver coffee server. As she lowered its spout to refill his cup, Case quickly covered it with his hand. "Oh, no, thank you, my dear. I'm fine."

He looked around. "Someone else?"

"Yes, a little here, please," requested Dare.

Morna moved to his end of the table.

"He met Riga at a music hall," Case resumed. "She was a dancer. Her parents were Romanian immigrants, Gypsies. She was only sixteen."

"Yes, that's young," agreed Dare. He moistened the tip of his finger and placed it on top of a large croissant crumb, pressed gently down, and then lifted the fallen crumb into his mouth. Morna was leaning over his cup. "And so how did he kill her?" Dare asked.

"Suffocation."

Dare emitted a yelp.

Morna gasped, her hand clapped over her mouth. Somehow missing Dare's cup, she had poured hot coffee onto his lap.

"Oh, I'm so sorry!"

Dare dabbed at the stain with his napkin.

"It's all right, love. I mean, really. Nothing to it. Not at all."

"You see, Morna?" said Case. "He forgives you."

She turned and met his odd, steady stare in silence; then she turned back away and uttered softly, "I know." While she filled

Dare's cup, her green gaze lifted up and for one intense moment met and held Trawley's.

"We're all fine here now, Morna," Case told her.

She nodded and moved off toward the kitchen.

"Getting back to the history of the house," resumed Case. He laid it out briefly: Built in 1937. Then in 1952 the murder of Riga and the death of Quandt himself minutes afterwards, apparently by his own hand. Ownership passed to a son, Regis Quandt, aged twelve when the tragedy occurred, and taken to live with Quandt's brother, Michael. Regis died when he was only twenty, mansion ownership passed to Michael and then finally to Michael's son, Paul Quandt. Meantime, the mansion had been put up for sale, but without success, and in 1954, and over the course of the next twenty years, was leased out any number of times, with the leases always broken through departure or death, including a period late in the fifties when the house had been occupied by a contemplative order of nuns who experienced an outbreak of "possession" hysteria reminiscent of three hundred years before among the nuns at the convent of Loudun in France. The nun in charge was found hanged from a wooden beam. "That was in 1958," said Case.

From then on, he explained, the house was unoccupied until 1984, when Paul Quandt, wealthy already from inheritance and now a historian of some note, moved in with his wife and three young children. Like others, they experienced the haunting phenomena, in particular deafening bangings on the outer walls. "And then there were other things..." said Case, his voice trailing off. He left it hanging. In 1987, he then recounted, the unnerving manifestations ceased, and so things remained until 1990, when the Quandts moved to Italy, decided they liked it there, and put the island and the mansion up for sale. But the house's reputation had outlived its reign of peace.

"Thus far," ended Case, "the tragic words of this ghastly gospel."

"So it all goes back to the wife being suffocated," said Dare.

"That's right," agreed Case.

"And so the wife is the ghost, is that the plot? Heavy breathing and moaning in the hallway at night? Perhaps the sound of someone tapping a pipe against his teeth?"

Subtly, Freeboard's middle finger lifted up in Dare's direction.

"I have no information that Quandt smoked a pipe, Mr. Dare," said Case, looking mildly at sea.

"Oh, you're saying that it's Quandt who haunts the place?"

"Perhaps so." Case reached out and plucked a chocolate from a small silver tray. "Most of the victims," he imparted, "have been women."

Dare paled. "Victims? What victims? You mean *dead* people?"

"Quite."

Freeboard sighed and then shifted in her chair.

"Are we going to talk about this forever?"

The realtor's eyes were glazed over with boredom.

"And of course, all these women died of fright," Dare said tightly.

"Only one. Three were suicides," said Case. "Two went insane."

The author turned his head and stared archly at Freeboard. "Some unscrupulous realtor, no doubt, kept leasing the place to loonies and chronic depressives."

"Mr. Dare, you sound defensive to me," observed Case. "Is it possible you secretly believe?"

"The suspension of *my* disbelief would require more cables than the Golden Gate Bridge."

"Yeah, Dare *is* doubt," Freeboard murmured, eyes hooded.

"Precisely. But merely for the sake of my article," said Dare, "even if there were such things as ghosts, why on earth don't they beetle on along to their reward instead of drifting and clotting around the old clubhouse making thoroughgoing pains in the ass of themselves?"

Case lifted an eyebrow. "Mrs. Trawley?"

But the psychic mutely demurred, lowering her eyes and shaking her head before again looking up at a sound from Freeboard as the realtor, with a heavy and impatient sigh, bowed down her head and closed her eyes; she'd awakened at approximately four that morning, after tossing and turning in a restless sleep. Case glanced at her unreadably, then turned to answer Dare. "Well, who knows?" he began. "But assume that when you die you're convinced—as you are, I presume, Mr. Dare—that death is the end of all consciousness. And then you die, but you remain fully conscious, so that the moment immediately after death seems no different from the one that came before. So in that case would it really be so terribly odd if there were some of us who simply didn't notice that we're dead?"

"I would notice," Dare insisted.

"Three months' notice," muttered Freeboard, half awake.

"Joan, I'm marking you absent," said Dare. He reached over and poked her in the side with a finger. Freeboard's head snapped up and her eyes opened wide. "Yeah, what's up?" she said, attempting to sound alert.

"Dr. Case was just implying that ghosts are nonbelievers; a rather nice irony, that, don't you think?"

"Yeah, that's great."

"Yes, I thought you might say that."

"Quit staring."

"I'm not staring."

"Yes, you are, Terry! Quit it!"

"I will."

The author returned his attention to Case.

"And so why wouldn't some sympathetic angel just come and tell these spirits to wake up and smell the coffee?" he asked.

"Good point. Perhaps they have to find it out for themselves."

"I think not knowing that you're dead is shocking ignorance, frankly."

"Maybe ghosts can't let go of their attachments," said Case.

"Lucky rocks," mentioned Freeboard.

Dare ignored it.

Case turned to Trawley and stared at her intently. "I meant mainly *emotional* attachments. Don't you think so, Mrs. Trawley? Or do you?"

Trawley lowered her eyes and shook her head. Softly, barely audibly, she said, "I don't know."

"What precisely *do* you know?" Dare demanded. "What is it, in fact, that you *do,* Mrs. Trawley? You're the quietest person I've ever met. Do you talk to the spirits, at least?"

The noted psychic stood up. "You'll excuse me just a moment?"

"Yes, of course," murmured Case. He looked embarrassed.

"You didn't say she was sensitive, you said *a* sensitive."

"Terry, you're a hemorrhoid," Freeboard told him quietly.

"I'm just going for some water," said the psychic, smiling thinly.

She opened a door and disappeared into the kitchen.

"I respect and adore you!" Dare called after her. "I kiss your ectoplasm."

"Shall we leave it at that, Mr. Dare?" Case suggested.

Freeboard glared. " 'I am doubt' could be 'I am dead.'"

* * *

IN THE KITCHEN, Trawley went to the double sink where Morna was standing washing dishes. "May I have a clean glass?" she asked. "I'd like some water."

Silently, the housekeeper rinsed her hands, dried them, then reached to the cupboard for a glass and began to fill it from the tap.

Trawley was staring at her intently.

"You've been with Dr. Case for many years?"

"Many years."

Morna's voice was colorless and quiet.

She turned off the tap and handed Trawley the glass.

"Such an awfully pleasant atmosphere to work in," said the psychic. "Dr. Case lives near the campus, does he, Morna?"

"Very near."

"And you?"

"Very far."

Morna had returned to the washing of the dishes.

"Oh, well, thank you for the water," Trawley told her.

"Yes."

For a moment Trawley stood there, silently staring, then abruptly she turned and walked out of the kitchen, quietly closing the door behind her. Hearing the sound, Morna turned and looked after her with unreadable ice-green eyes.

When Trawley retook her seat at the table, Case and Dare were still arguing over ghosts and Freeboard was again half asleep in her chair. "Dr. Case," Dare was saying, "with all due respect to your learning and intelligence, am I gathering correctly that you've actually made up your mind that ghosts in fact exist?"

"Mr. Dare," Case replied, "with all respect to your literary genius, I'm proposing that the mechanistic, clockwork universe of materialistic science is probably the greatest superstition of our age. Do you know what the quantum physicists are telling us? They're saying now that atoms aren't things, they're really 'processes,' and that matter is a kind of illusion; that electrons are capable of moving from place to place without traversing the space in between and that positrons actually are electrons that appear to be traveling backwards in time and that subatomic particles can communicate over a distance of trillions of miles without there being any causal connection between them. Do ghosts exist? Are they here with us now? In this room? Right beside you, perhaps? Who can say? But in a world like the one that I've just described, can there really be a place for a thing like surprise?"

As Dare was considering this statement, a soft but distinct, clear rap was heard. All eyes shifted to the center of the oaken table; it was as if it had been struck by an invisible knuckle. For moments no one spoke and the only sound was the patter of the rain on the mullioned windows. Then at last, beneath her breath, Freeboard murmured, "Shit!"

Trawley eyed her with a look of fond indulgence.

Dare cleared his throat and sat up in his chair. His gaze remained fixed on the center of the table as he asked, "Have you ever *seen* a ghost, Dr. Case?"

"Oh, I see them constantly."

Dare looked up and saw that Case was smiling. "Oh, come on now, let's have a straight answer," he chided. "Have you ever seen a ghost?"

"Carl Jung, the great psychiatrist, saw one."

"You jest, sir."

"No, he saw one right beside him in his bed."

"Oh, well, some people will say anything at all to get published."

"Jung suspected that the dead aren't really in a different place at all from the living,"

Case went on, "but in fact were in some sort of parallel state that coexists alongside our world but remains unseen because it exists at a higher frequency, like the blades of a propeller or a fan."

"You mean the afterlife is just another alternative lifestyle?"

Case smiled, put his head down and shook it. "Mr. Dare!"

"Doggie bow-wow," Freeboard murmured with a soft, lilting menace. Then she grimaced, briefly crossing her eyes, while her finger made a rapid slashing move across her throat. Dare shifted hooded eyes to her briefly, then ignored her. "Dr. Case," he said, "assuming the preposterous for a moment, what on earth makes you think that any ghost is going to act up on cue just because we're all here on this mission?"

"Oh, no solid reason, really." Case shrugged. "But I've charted all the really nasty happenings at Elsewhere, and, oddly, as it happens, almost all of them occurred at the same time of year."

"So when is that?" Freeboard asked. She was stifling a yawn.

"Sometime in June. Early June. In fact, right about now."

No one spoke. The only sound was the scraping of Case's spoon against the porcelain bottom of his cup as he stirred his coffee in an absent gesture. Freeboard shot a wary glance to Dare, appraising him, and felt an incipient rush of dismay as she couldn't discern that he was actually breathing. But at last he cleared his throat. "These people that you said went insane," he asked Case without a trace of his customary mocking tone: "Are they living? Is it possible they could be interviewed?"

"Yes, there is one who is still alive—Sara Casey. She's in Bellevue Psychiatric at the moment. The poor woman is completely unbalanced, I'm afraid. She insists that at Elsewhere malevolent entities are living in the spaces in the walls."

The author turned to Freeboard with a bloodless surmise.

"*Hollow* walls?" he intoned.

Case nodded.

Freeboard flipped the Phantom mask into Dare's face.

THE BRUNCH ENDED, Anna Trawley was back in her room. She sat on the edge of the bed in quiet reverie, staring at the silver-framed photo of a dimpled young girl that she held in her lap with still hands. Fleeting shadows of the rain's trickling currents on a window crept weakly down the paleness of her face like

dying prayers. At last she propped the photo
on a nightstand by her bed. She'd already
placed a miniature alarm clock there, a perfect
square with sides of smooth shiny brass and
red numerals; she had bought it while working
in Switzerland during the search for a serial
killer. She noted the time: 1:14. Case and Dare
were still talking downstairs when she'd left
them and Freeboard had gone to her room
to rest. She stood up and walked over to a
narrow writing desk beneath a rain-spattered
gabled window, pulled out the straight-backed
wooden chair, sat down, and then reached a
pale hand into the drawer of the desk and
from within it fetched a silvery ink-fed pen
and a diary bound in soft pink leather; in the
center of the cover a floral design of lavender
blossoms entwined in a circle. Trawley
unsheathed the point of the pen, and with
slender, short fingers she opened the diary; it
was new and emitted a faint, quick whiff of
glue and new-made paper. At the top of the
blank first page she wrote "Elsewhere" in a
large and rounded, elegant script. Her pen
made a tiny scratching sound. She turned in
her chair to check the clock, and then at the
top of the next clean page she recorded the
day, the date and the time. Below that she
carefully penned an entry:

FINALLY, I AM AT *Elsewhere. Forbidding
from without, within it is warm. And yet
something feels broken here, awry, though
I haven't any inkling of what it could be.
Joan Freeboard, the realtor, is an original,
I am fond of her already; she seems to
make me smile inside. And though it
might shock him to know it, perhaps, I
do find that I like Terence Dare as well;
so amusing, so wounded at his core, like
the world. Dr. Case, as expected, is quite
professorial. He is also quite smashingly
handsome. Yet I'm sensing an aura
of danger about him, as well as some
mystery that he exudes. I felt it when
the housekeeper, Morna, appeared. He
seemed somehow taken aback. Why was
that? And then again when he pointed
me out to her and said, "Mrs. Trawley
is clairvoyant, Morna." He said it very
pointedly, I thought. And then something
else: when we arrived he said, "There
you all are again." What on earth could
he possibly have meant by that? It could
be that he misspoke, I suppose; likely so.
I feel myself attracted to the man, I must
say; I suppose that's why I had to get a
closer look at Morna. (I still can't believe
I was poking around to find out if the girl
was a "live-in." Shameless!) But I find I'm*

*unable to penetrate Case: my impressions
are as stones flung and skimming off the
surface of a pond in whose depths some
Leviathan lurks, some puzzle that has to
be solved—and yet mustn't. I see I am
wandering, making no sense. The trip has
been hard on my bones, so exhausting,
and I'm feeling disconnected, as if in
a dream. Perhaps a little lie-down will
clear away the foggies. Dreams. How I
dread them; I always wake up. Who was
it in Shakespeare who "cried to dream
again"?*

TRAWLEY LOOKED UP at the rain-streaked
window, pensive, her eyes pools of memory
and sadness; then abruptly she turned to her
left and listened. Immobile, she waited, head
tilted to the side. Then it seemed as if a tremor
had bolted through the room, the lone strike
of an earthquake, faint but sharp. The psychic
held still and continued to listen. Then she
lowered her head to the diary and wrote:

PERHAPS THERE IS *something going on
here after all. Either that, or I am losing
my senses completely. I have just heard the
voice of a man speaking Latin. Here. In this*

room. Not sensed—heard. *I can translate the words, but I don't understand them:
"I cast you out, unclean spirit..."*

DOWNSTAIRS IN THE comfortable, teak-paneled library crammed with books and mementos of travel, Gabriel Case adjusted a television set as Dare watched him from a downy sofa. "Getting nothing but static," murmured Case with annoyance.

There was no picture on the screen, only "snow."

"Try another channel," prompted Dare.

"I've tried them all."

Case flipped through more channels, and then turned off the set. He sat down on the sofa facing Dare. "Perhaps it's the storm," he observed. "At least I hope so. We'd never get a repairman to come over here. Never."

Dare glowered. "I wish you'd try not to say things like that."

"What's the difference? Nothing's happened here in years."

"No one's *been* here in years."

"Quite so. Like a drink? We've got everything." Case gestured toward a built-in bar in the corner made of dark-stained oak that was shiny with wax. Four ornately carved oaken stools stained to match were arranged along the gentle curve of the counter.

Dare shook his head. "Much too early. My God, it's barely three." He checked his watch. "Eight minutes after."

"Would you like to hear the story of Jung and his ghost?"

Case was innocently staring, hands folded on his stomach.

"You have a dangerous and sly sense of humor, Dr. Case."

"The story's fascinating. Don't you want to hear it?"

"I would sooner be in Bosnia-Herzegovina eating sushi with Muslims in an old Russian tank."

Dare stood up. "I must make a few notes. You'll forgive me?"

Without further ado the author strode from the room. Case watched him walk stiffly to the staircase, ascend it, and finally vanish into his room. Case sighed and bent his head and then looked up to his left as a long and jagged fissure in the wall opened up, deep and wide, with a crackling of plaster and wood. Case watched without expression, silent and ummoving, as the massive gap sealed itself up without a trace. Then he lowered his head and gently shook it.

"Bad timing," he murmured.

A tremor shook the room.

"Bloody nuisance as well," Case grumbled. "It's the left hand not knowing what the right hand is doing."

He waited for another disturbance. But nothing else came.

Not yet.

CHAPTER FOUR

Y OU'RE ALL RIGHT?" Case asked.

"Yes, I'm fine," Trawley murmured.

"Watch your step there just ahead."

"Oh, yes, thank you."

They had entered by the alcove door beneath the staircase, descending stone steps to a concrete passageway that was narrow and dank and dark. Case shone a powerful flashlight beam on the ground just ahead to illuminate the way.

"There aren't any lights down here?" Trawley asked. Above her dress she wore a thin tan cardigan sweater. "Seems there ought to be," she gently complained.

"They're here. They don't work for some reason."

"No."

"In here. Watch your head, Mrs. Trawley."

"I will."

He led her through a doorway into a small rectangular chamber. "Well, we're here," he announced, and they stopped. He lifted the flashlight beam to a structure, an ornamental gray stone crypt just ahead of them. Carved into the front of it, glaring in fury, was a hideous and gaping demonic face identical to that on the door above.

"This is the heart of the house," Case intoned.

The psychic made no comment. He turned to her.

"That was meant to make you laugh," he said quietly. "It's what they say in haunted house movies."

"I know," Trawley said. "My heart smiled."

"It should do that more often."

Case centered the light beam on the gargoylish face. "Pretty creature," he observed sardonically.

"How hideous. That's where he buried her?"

"Not exactly," answered Case.

"Not exactly?"

"He sealed her up inside while she was still alive."

Trawley winced. "Dear God," she murmured.

"Brutal bastard. Forgive my French."

Trawley moved slowly forward and then lightly brushed a hand along the face of the crypt.

"Can you see?" Case inquired.

"Very well."

He came up beside here.

"Is Quandt in here too?" she asked him.

"Yes," replied Case. "He is here."

"How did he die?"

"Chironex fleckeri."

Trawley stopped feeling at the crypt and turned around to him. She couldn't see him, his face was a darkness.

"That's Latin," she said softly.

"It's the venom of the sea anemone. They discovered a vial of its dregs in his hand. Here. On this spot. The venom paralyzes the vocal cords, and then the respiratory system, and in an hour the victim is dead from suffocation."

Trawley put a hand to her neck. "Oh, how horrible."

"Yes."

"Why would he choose such a painful way to die?"

"God knows."

She stared at his silhouette for a moment, then turned again to look at the crypt. "Bizarre design. You said the house dates from 1937?"

"Yes. But this was here first. Before. There was once another house on this site."

"Is that so?"

"Edward Quandt tore it down and rebuilt."

"But he left this crypt untouched?"

"He did."

"And who was buried here then?"

"Or what."

Once again she turned her head to his voice. She could see him more clearly now, though his eyes were still shadowed and hidden.

"I've found mentions in his diary of something," Case said quietly. "Some overwhelmingly cruel and malevolent..." He paused, as though searching for a word; then said "...presence."

In the hush that followed, a fragment of plaster broke loose from a wall. It trickled to the floor. Case turned his head to the sound, listening; then after a moment turned back to look at Trawley. "Do you sense something, Anna?" he asked her.

"Why?"

"The way you're staring."

"You seem so familiar to me."

"Really?"

"Yet I know we've never met," Trawley mused.

"Perhaps in some other lifetime," said Case.

"Exactly. But past or future?"

Trawley turned again to look at the crypt, then she shivered and started to button her sweater as she faced around again and looked down. "Let's go back. I've caught a chill," she said.

"Oh, I'm so sorry."

He tilted the flashlight's beam to the ground just ahead, and together they exited the chamber and slowly walked back toward the steps leading up.

"Do you really believe in past lives, Dr. Case?"

"Need we really be so formal?"

"Very well," she said. "Gabriel."

"Good."

"Do you believe?" she repeated.

"I agree with Voltaire."

"Who said what?"

"That the concept of being born twice is really no more surprising than being born once."

She turned her head. His face was still shrouded in darkness, yet now she could see him much better.

"HEY, TERRY!"

"You called, my dove?"

"Yeah, come in here a second, wouldjya?"

Freeboard was sitting at a desk in the library working with a small electronic calculator and a stack of recent real estate statistics. She wore thick-lensed reading glasses. Dare was in the Great Room in front of a stereo cabinet reading an album cover as Artie Shaw's "Begin the Beguine" warmed the air. "What is it?" he called out. "Too loud? Do you want me to turn down the music?"

"No, I like it. Just get in here a second, Terry, would you?"

Dare placed the album down and approached. He wore jeans, a camel sweater and new white tennis shoes. He reached the desk and looked down at the realtor. She continued to work at the calculator.

"You're all fresh-eyed and loathsomely alert," he remarked.

"Took a snooze. God, this Case must be getting to me, Terry. I dreamed I left my body and went traveling."

"To where? Some construction site?"

"I dunno. Someplace dark. A dark box."

"Could be worse. So what's up, my dear? What's on your mind?"

"Today a holiday or something, Terry?"

"Why?"

"You tried calling anybody?"

"Don't the phones work?" he asked.

"Yeah, they work," she replied, "but I can't get anyone to answer."

"Don't be silly. How on earth would they know who was calling?"

She looked up at him dismally for a moment, then returned to her work. "You can be such an asshole at times."

"It's a gift."

"I've called the office nine times now," she told him, "and the phone just keeps ringing and ringing. No service, no voice mail, no nothing." She nodded her head toward a telephone receiver that lay on its side atop the desk. "You hear that? Twenty minutes."

Dare picked up the receiver, put it to his ear and heard the distant, steady ringing at the end of the line. He frowned, then put the phone gently back on the desk. "Oh, well, it could be a bomb scare or something."

"Or not. Same thing happens when I try to get an operator. *Shit!*" She ripped off a length of computer tape and crumpled it up in her fist. "Now I've got to do the freaking thing over!"

Dare stood pondering silently with his head down, his hands deep down in the pockets of his jeans. "God, I really miss the dogs," he said wanly.

Freeboard punched at the calculator rapidly.

"Times one-oh-point seven two…"

Dare looked up as if in sudden realization and dismay.

"The dogs!" he exclaimed. "I forgot to bring the dogs!"

"No, you brought them," said Freeboard.

Dare frowned, looking puzzled and uncertain. "No, the dogs aren't here. I must have left them behind."

"I could swear that you brought them," Freeboard murmured distractedly as she punched in another set of numbers.

Uneasy, Dare looked down at the telephone receiver. "Begin the Beguine" had just ended, there was silence and the ringing at the end of the line seemed more resonant now, although somehow even farther away. Dare shook his head and bit his lip, then spoke quietly.

"How on earth could I have forgotten the dogs?"

CHAPTER FIVE

TRAWLEY SIPPED TEA laced with sugar and milk as she stared out the window almost touching her shoulder where splatters of rain fell in random strikes. "How long is this predicted to last? Have you heard?"

Case followed her gaze and shook his head. "No, I haven't. There's still no reception on radio or television."

"Oh."

"Must be the storm. I'm getting nothing but static."

Trawley turned to study his face. "Me too."

He looked around and met her gaze. They were sitting across from each other at a table in a windowed nook of the breakfast room that was tucked away just off the kitchen. Case gripped the handle of the porcelain teapot. "More?"

The psychic shook her head and said, "No."

He poured for himself and then plucked two sugar cubes from a bowl. They made a crisply papery sound as he unwrapped them. "And so what do you make of all this?"

"Make of what?"

"This whole thing." Case plopped the cubes into the teacup and stirred. "Miss Freeboard seems bored beyond terminal ennui," he went on, "yet she pressed me to take this thing on."

"Oh, well, yes. She did the same thing with me."

"She told me she was doing it as an enormous favor for a friend.

"Forgotten his name. Oh, yes, Redmund, I think," recalled Case. "James Redmund."

"Oh."

"Why 'Oh'?"

"Well, Mr. Dare was going on about some friend of Miss Freeboard's for quite a little while in the limo driving up. Said he'd 'seen better faces on a totem pole in Maui?' Could that be the same person, I wonder? Smokes a pipe?"

"I don't know. Miss Freeboard told me that he'd begged her to put this thing together. Did she tell you that, too, by any chance?"

"Not exactly. She said if it turned out that the house is haunted, she could never in good conscience make a sale at *any* price."

"No, of course not," Case agreed with a shake of the head.

Their eyes met earnestly for a moment, and then suddenly they broke into laughter together. "Oh, I suppose we'll get the truth of it one of these days," said Trawley as their chuckling tapered to smiles.

"Yes, I'm sure that we will one day. So we will."

Suddenly the tempo of the rain picked up. Trawley turned to look out but the rain was slashing and the arbor of trees beyond was blurred. "Reminds me of a science fiction story I once read," she mused. "About a planet where it never stopped raining. That could surely put an edge on, couldn't it?"

"Yes."

"Tell me, how did you get into this field?"

"Through death."

She turned her head and found him brooding out the window.

"The death of someone close to me," Case said very softly. "Someone that I loved

103

more than life...more than myself. I grew obsessed with somehow proving to myself that she hadn't been utterly extinguished. Dear God, is there any pain of loss more keen than that one? I don't believe that I'd ever felt farther from the sun." He turned and met Trawley's gaze for a moment, and then looked toward the Great Room sadly. "No Cole Porter," he noted. "Too bad. I was getting quite attached to it, really."

He looked down into his teacup. "Oh, I'd always theoretically believed in the soul. Matter cannot reflect upon itself. But my grief needed more than that, it needed evidence."

"And so here you are trying to prove that there are ghosts."

Case looked up into her eyes with a warm, slight smile.

"Do you think I'll succeed, Anna?"

"Yes. I think you will."

Abruptly the rain slackened off to a patter.

"And what of you, Anna?"

"Me?"

"Yes, how did you come by your gift?"

"My gift?" She said it with a trace of bitter irony.

"You said that very oddly," Case observed.

Trawley stared out the window.

"My gift," she said dully.

"Yes, how did you come by it, Anna? By the way, there's an ancient Egyptian version of Genesis in which God says repeatedly to Adam, 'You were once a bright angel,' then describes how he and Eve have been stripped of the faculties of telepathy and knowledge at a distance. Perhaps it was natural to us once. Were you born with it, Anna?"

She turned and stared down at her tea.

"No," she said softly. "I wasn't born with it at all. It came when I'd suffered a severe concussion. I was driving my four-year-old daughter to school. The road was icy. I skid and hit a pole. She was killed."

"Oh, I'm so terribly sorry."

The psychic looked up, staring off with concern.

"Someone's frightened. I'm feeling someone's terror."

"He'll be fine," said Case.

Trawley turned and searched his eyes inscrutably.

"What was that?" she asked.

"Oh, I'm just guessing."

"Guessing what?"

"That you're sensing our esteemed Mr. Dare. I really think he's half frightened to death."

"Yes, that could be."

Case's brow knitted slightly. "He asked me if he'd brought along two little dogs. What a question!"

"Yes, he asked me that, too."

"What did you tell him?"

She looked suddenly blank.

Case waited, and then turned to another subject.

"Have you ever tried reaching your daughter?"

"Yes, I have."

"With success?"

"I don't know. I reached someone."

"You're not sure of it?"

"Dead people lie. They're just people."

He leaned back and pressed his palms against the edge of the table. "How amazing you should say that!" he declared.

"Well, it's true."

"No, I meant it confirms something for me."

"Really."

Case seemed to grow energized; his eyes sparkled. "There's a fascinating book by a Latvian scientist named Raudieve who claimed to hear voices of the dead on a tape recorder. It's called *Breakthrough: Electronic Communication with the Dead*. Do you know of it?"

"I've heard of it."

"Right. The author says more or less the same thing as you: that the dead know no more than when they were alive and gave false and often contradictory answers to his questions."

Trawley nodded.

"The voices were faint," Case went on, "and quite fleeting, almost buried under amplifier noise, and with a strange and unexpected lilting rhythm. Some moaned and said 'Help me' and seemed tormented. Others seemed content, even happy. Raudieve heard one voice that he was able to recognize, an old colleague from medical school. Raudieve asked him to describe his situation in a word or two—the voices are so difficult to hear and detect—and he answered distinctly, 'I'm in class.' Is this striking you as balmy, by the way?"

Trawley gently shook her head but her eyes smiled faintly.

Case went on: "Another time Raudieve asked—of no one in particular, he says— 'What is the purpose of your present existence?' and he heard back very clearly, 'Learning to be happy.' What a statement! When I read it I got the strong feeling that what Raudieve was in touch with was precisely the afterlife described by C. S. Lewis in *The Great Divorce*, with the dead being all in the same place, really; it's how they perceive it makes it heaven or hell; and their perception is shaped by how they've lived their earthly lives." He looked down and shook his head. "I don't know. When Raudieve asked where they were, he heard a voice answer clearly, 'Doctor Angels'; then there came another voice that said, 'It's like a hospital.' And then later someone answered, 'Limbo.'

"It's the Disturbed Ward of a lunatic asylum."

Case glanced up at the psychic. He looked puzzled.

Trawley was staring at him intently.

"And some of the inmates," she finished, "are dangerous."

Case held her gaze without expression, unblinking.

"Yes, no doubt," he said finally.

"No doubt."

"Getting back to Raudieve and the tapes..."

"Oh, yes, do."

"He gave up the experiments when the voices grew threatening. But before that he'd asked them, 'Does God exist?' and back came the answer, 'Not in the dream world.' When I read that it chilled me for some reason. Don't know why. Then it suddenly occurred to me that the dream world wasn't there—it was *this* one."

For a time Case probed the psychic's eyes. She broke the silence.

"Did you ever remarry?" she asked.

Case said, "No."

Bright yellow sunlight shafted through the window.

They turned their heads and stared out at the sky.

"Ah, sun. The storm's broken," said Case.

"So it has."

"The sky's a wonder after rain, don't you think? There really are some very lovely things about this world. Sometimes we tend to grow attached to its griefs."

Trawley turned to him. Color had risen in her face.

"What do you mean?"

Case shrugged and stared down at the table. "I once heard of a woman addicted to surgery. She had endless unneeded operations. Not in a masochistic way, you understand. She'd simply grown attached to the pain. She couldn't bear to be without it for too long. It had become her very reason for existence."

He looked up and met her riveted gaze.

"We'll have a séance later?" he asked her.

Trawley looked flustered and ill at ease.

"Very possibly," she answered him tersely. "We'll see."

Case turned to the window, staring out thoughtfully, and his brow began to wrinkle a little as he nodded and murmured to himself, "Perhaps we should. Yes, maybe this time we should try something new."

Trawley stared. "'This time,' did you say?"

Case turned to her blankly. "I'm sorry?"

"You said, 'This time.' What did you mean by that?"

Case looked foggy. "I haven't a clue. My mind wandered."

She stared at him steadily. "Yes. That happens to me, too."

"I'm so sorry."

She picked up her teacup.

"So you teach at Columbia," she commented.

"Yes."

"Such a stimulating atmosphere to work in. Do you live near the campus, by chance?"

"No, I commute," said Case. "Why do you ask?"

"Oh, just curious, that's all. No special reason." Trawley sipped at her tea, and as she set down her cup it made a tiny but prolonged faint clattering sound against the brittle porcelain of the saucer. Case darted a glance to the cup, her trembling hands. She lowered them swiftly to her lap and out of sight. After a moment Case lifted his gaze.

"You're still worried about Dare?" he asked quietly.

"Yes," said Trawley. "I'm worried about all of us, really."

"Don't be concerned," Case told her.

"Why not?"

"Nothing ever seems to happen here until dark."

"BOYS? WHERE ARE YOU, my babies? Are you here?"

Lost and forlorn, confused, frightened, Dare made his way slowly along a hallway. Setting out to find his dogs, he had entered the hall from which Morna had first been seen to emerge, and in moving from hall to connecting hall he'd soon found himself wandering in a maze and completely unable to retrace his steps.

He opened a door and looked into a bedroom.

"Boys? Are you here? Maria? Pompette?"

Through a window sunlight sifted into the room, thin and filtered through the branches of giant oaks. A narrow beam had found its way unbroken to a bureau. Dare stared; he thought it odd that no dust motes danced within it. The next instant the dust motes appeared in the beam, swirling swiftly in a spiraling Brownian movement. For a moment Dare contemplated this event, then dismissed it and again called out softly, "Here, boys!"

He heard an ominous creaking sound from the hall, like that of a single, tentative footstep, and then the sound of a door closing quietly somewhere. Dare held his breath. He stepped out into the hallway and looked down its length. Nothing. He exhaled, then carefully moved down the hall again. "Come on, boys! Maria Hidalgo? Pompette?" He made smacking summoning sounds with his lips.

Dare came to another door and stopped, but as he was about to push it open he heard yet another strange sound from somewhere. At first it sounded like the distant buzzing of bees, but then as Dare stood motionless, straining to hear, it became a low murmuring, indistinct and run together, of several men speaking—praying?—in Latin. Confounded, Dare stopped and attentively listened and then saw something moving at the end of the hall, a black shape. He saw it open the door of a room at the end of the hall, walk into it, and close the door behind it. The author's eyes widened. And then suddenly he leaped from his skin with a yelp as from behind him a hand came down on his shoulder. Dare whirled, his heart pounding.

"Oh, there you are," said Gabriel Case. He was standing there, smiling indulgently. "Mr. Dare, I've been searching for you everywhere. Really. Exploring the house, are we?"

"Yes. I mean, no."

The author put a hand to his chest to still his heart.

"My God, I'm awfully glad to see you," he exhaled with relief.

"I had a feeling that that might be the case."

"I got lost."

"Not so difficult to do in this house: it's disordered, no sense to where anything lies or leads. Come along," urged Case, "we're right this way." He opened a door and led Dare into yet another hallway.

"We've been missing you," he said.

"I've been missing a tall brandy-soda. Incidentally, what's that priest doing here?"

"What priest?"

"How would *I* know? Boris Karloff's old chaplain!" Dare expostulated. "I just saw him down the hall back there."

Case halted. "Are you serious?"

"Please don't do that to me, Doctor."

"Call me Gabriel," said Case.

"I said *stop* that!"

"Doctor," Case quietly amended.

"Thank you. I thought I heard this murmuring and mumbling in Latin, then I saw this tall priest walking by. You mean you don't know who he is?"

Case mulled it over, then again began to walk. Dare followed.

"Are you Catholic, Mr. Dare?"

"Ex-Catholic."

"Is there actually any such thing?"

"What's your point?"

"We're all alerted to seeing *something* in this house," Case said soothingly. "Our unconscious expectations have been heightened. And you've heard me say some nuns were once exorcised here."

"You're suggesting I've had a papally induced hallucination?"

"I'm suggesting that you're more of a believer than you say, and saw shadows, or, more likely, that you're sending me up. Can you tell me which it is, Mr. Dare?"

"Let's find a drink."

ANNA TRAWLEY CHECKED the time, sat down at the desk and then penned a new entry into her diary. She wrote:

IT'S 5:23 P.M. *I am shaken and not certain as to why I had tea with Case. My attraction grows stronger. And yet so does my sense that he is somehow a peril to me, to my soul, to my very life. When I'm near him I tremble. Isn't that absurd? God help me, I simply cannot figure it out. Am I dotty? Yes, of course, that might explain almost everything. How easy to become insane. And yet certain odd puzzles are not of my imagining. He and Morna don't agree on where he lives: one says close to the Columbia campus, and the other—Case himself—says far, far away. It's too bizarre. Perhaps one of them—the girl, I would think—misunderstood me. But that's a minor matter. The main thing is my instincts are crying out danger. And not merely from Case. I continue hearing voices, threatening, angry. I know I'm not imagining them. They are here.*

CHAPTER SIX

SMOTHERING, SHRIEKING IN terror, trapped in a narrow dry prison of night, Freeboard wakened abruptly from a brief, light doze and sat up on the bed with a whimpering cry. She put a hand to her forehead. It was chilly and damp. "Shit, that stupid dream *again*!" she muttered. She waited, then at last she swung her legs off the bed, stood up, trudged into the bathroom, turned on a tap and splashed cold water onto her face. Drying off with a towel, she looked in the mirror. Get a hold! she admonished herself. It didn't work. The dream was recurring and always disturbed her, yet she couldn't remember when she'd started to have it. Involuntarily, she shivered. She needed to be out of this room, to be with people. She hurried from the bathroom, picked up a clean ashtray and banged it once sharply against the wall. "You in there, dickhead?"

Freeboard waited. Nothing. Silence. She put back the ashtray, strode to the door and walked out into the hall. There she looked up and down but saw no one. It's so quiet, she thought. She walked to the railing and glanced down at the Great Room. It was empty and still. The sconce lights were on.

"Terry?"

Freeboard waited. Then she heard something, voices, to her right. They were low and murmury, indistinct. She turned toward the sound. It was coming from the long empty hall that ran past Dare's and Trawley's rooms. At the end was a door. Freeboard stared at it, puzzled, then strode toward it purposefully as she heard the low voices again; they seemed to be coming from that direction. She got to the door and pushed it open, and as she did the voices ceased and there was sudden, deep silence. Freeboard frowned. She was peering down a long windowless corridor at the end of which stood another door. "Terry, you flaming asshole," she called, "is that you screwing around in there?" Freeboard heard a door softly closing behind her. Turning quickly, she saw Trawley coming out of her room. The psychic saw her and approached, looking tense and troubled. "Something in there?" she asked. She was looking past Freeboard into the darkened inner hall.

"No."

Freeboard closed the hall door.

"Joan, I thought I'd take a stroll around the island. Want to come?"

"Yes, I'd like that a lot," said Freeboard. "Yes!"

It would prove to be no ordinary walk on the beach.

"YOUR HEALTH," toasted Case.

"You keep saying that," said Dare.

The author's voice was faintly thickened and slurry.

They were sitting across from one another on the library sofas, close to the crackling of a fire. Case was leaning across a pine coffee table pouring scotch into Dare's tall glass.

"No one's forcing you to drink," Case observed.

"I wasn't bitching, I was merely observing; that's a thing that we painters can do so awfully well."

"Oh, you paint?"

"Must you challenge almost everything I say?"

Slightly inebriated, feeling loose, the author sipped at his glass and savored the scotch. And then the earth seemed to shift in a quick, sharp jolt. Dare lowered his glass and stared.

"I think a sumo wrestler just landed on the island," he intoned.

He looked over at Case. "Did you feel that?"

"Feel what?"

"Never mind." Dare kicked off his shoes, swung his long legs around and stretched out full on the sofa. "There. I am invulnerable, I hold back the night. You may now tell me more about Carl Jung's ghost."

"Really?"

"Oh, yes, really, sir. Indeed. My very word."

"Well, it looked like a one-eyed old hag," began Case. "Jung was looking for a place to relax for a time, and a friend of his in London—another doctor, I believe—offered use of his cottage in the country. One beautiful moonlit night with no wind as he lay in bed, Jung said he heard trickling sounds, odd creaks, and then muffled bangings on the outer walls. Then he had the strong feeling that someone was near him and so he opened his eyes and immediately saw, there beside him on the pillow, the hideous face of an elderly woman, her right eye wide open and balefully glaring at him from just a few inches away. The left half of the face, he said, was missing below the eye. Jung leaped up and out of bed, lit a number of candles and spent the rest of the night out of doors on a cot he'd dragged out of the house. Later on he found the cottage that he was vacationing in had long been known to be haunted and was formerly owned by an elderly woman who had died from a cancerous lesion of the eye."

"I had to ask," muttered Dare.

"Yes, there you have it."

Dare reached out, retrieved his glass and sipped. He stared at the fireplace flames as if in a reverie. "I may have had a taste of the supernatural once," he said in a quiet tone. "I was in Budapest doing some research. I knew few people. I was lonely. On the morning of my fortieth birthday I went to the lobby and in my box there was a cablegram, my only mail in several days. It said 'Happy Birthday, dear Terry' and at the bottom it was signed, 'Your brother, Ray.'" Dare paused and looked down into his glass and swirled the scotch. "Oh, yes, I had a brother Raymond," he said after that. "But he died, you see, in infancy. Another brother had sent me the cable. Edward. But how on earth did Edward turn into Ray?"

The author held his glass out to Case.

"May we hear 'To your health' one more time?"

"You need ice?"

"I need warmth, my dear man, I need fire. Just the scotch. The world is quite cold enough for me, thank you."

Case picked up the bottle. Its treasure had dwindled and he poured it all out into the author's glass.

"Forgive me for asking, Mr. Dare—or rather, Terence. You don't mind if I call you that?"

"I'd say about time."

Case set the empty bottle down and leaned back.

"May I ask you a personal question?"

"Has it anything to do with LSD?"

"I don't think so."

"Or priests?"

"Oh, well, possibly priests."

Dare glared. "Henri Bergson thought the principal function of the brain was to filter out most of reality so that we could focus on the tasks of earthly life," he said. "When the filter is weakened by a powerful drug, what we see is not delusion but the truth."

"I haven't followed you," said Case.

"I saw the priest," insisted Dare.

"Oh, I see. No, that's not what I meant."

"Then what is?"

"What sent you away from your church?"

For a moment there was silence. Dare gulped down the scotch and stared into the fire. "All that rot about eternal hell's fires and damnation. Just because I like Mackinaws more than silk blouses, I'm condemned to take baths in jalapeño juice and eat napalm hot fudge sundaes with Son of Sam for all of eternity in some Miltonesque Jack in the Box? Is hell fair?"

"No, no one said that it was fair," said Case quickly.

"Well, it isn't."

"In any case, you're over that now."

"Absolutely. Dead is dead and that's that."

"So there we are. Oh, incidentally—one more thing about that one-eyed old ghost..."

Dare lowered his brow into a hand. "Ah, my God!"

"You find this threatening?"

"No, my fingernails *always* look charred. It's some sort of genetic balls-up in my family."

"I see."

Dare looked up and set his glass down on the table.

"You were saying?"

"Well, the ghost spoke to Jung."

"Good *Christ*!"

Case looked slightly bemused, a little grave.

"And what did it say?" Dare asked.

"'When you have learned to forgive others, Jung, you will finally learn to forgive yourself.'"

Dare paled. He seemed taken aback.

"It really said that?"

Case was staring at him steadily. He shook his head. "No."

"You're a dangerous man, Dr. Case," Dare said softly. "I've said that before. Yes, you are. You're a peril."

Case turned and looked out through a window. The shadows of the trees were beginning to lengthen, and the sound of birds calling were fewer, more muted.

"The sun's lower," he said softly. "I'm impatient for the night."

"PRETTY SKY," said Trawley.

"It's a sky." Freeboard shrugged.

They had sauntered through the oaks around the house and now were ambling by the evening river's glistening shore where the sun had laid a gold piece on the surface of the waters. Her tanned arms folded across her chest, the realtor seemed pensive, staring down at the ground.

"Something wrong, Joan?"

"Huh-uh."

"You seem edgy."

"No, I'm fine. I'm just thinking."

"What about?"

At that moment she'd been pondering her dream of the angel, the one with the memorable name unremembered and his cryptic admonition, "The clams aren't safe." Before that she'd been thinking of Amy O'Donnell from the second grade at St. Rose in the Bronx. Her best friend. Dead at nine. Pneumonia. "Nothing special. Business. I dunno." Freeboard shrugged. A moment later she stopped and looked up. She was squinting toward the sun, her browed furrowed.

"You hear that?"

"No, what?"

"Sounds like organ music. Listen."

Trawley followed her gaze, her head bent.

"Yes, I do," she said shortly. "Far away."

"Yeah, I guess there's a skating rink somewhere."

"Perhaps."

Freeboard nodded and the women resumed their walk.

"So there's Manhattan," said Trawley, looking off to the south. "I've never spent any time there to speak of," she mentioned. "Perhaps I should do that before I go home. What do you think? Is it a fascinating city?"

"Fuck it."

"You don't recommend it, then?" Trawley asked earnestly.

Freeboard turned her head to unreadably appraise her. The psychic's expression was somberly questioning, but her eyes seemed faintly amused. "You're okay," Freeboard judged her at last.

"I'm okay?"

"Yeah, that's right. You're okay. You're real."

Both hands in the pockets of her jeans, thumbs hitched, Freeboard turned and frowned down at the ground ahead. "Listen, what's the bottom line?" she asked. "I mean, spookwise."

"Beg your pardon?"

"Hey, look at this," Freeboard said abruptly. She had stopped, staring down at a sand-covered object that looked as if it might have washed up on the shore. She stooped and picked it up.

It was a bottle of champagne.

Freeboard brushed away sand and read the faded, blurred label.

"Veuve Cliquot," she pensively murmured.

Trawley eyed the bottle. She looked troubled.

"Unopened," she observed.

"Yeah, it is."

Freeboard looked up and Trawley followed her gaze to where the shoreline just ahead sharply curved to the right, disappearing from view. The two women stood immobile, blankly staring. A light spring breeze played at Trawley's dress for a moment, furling and flapping it about. Freeboard lowered her hand and the champagne bottle slipped from her fingers down to the silent and watching earth. Then as one the women turned and walked stiffly toward the mansion.

Neither of them uttered a word.

ON THE LIBRARY sofa Dare lay somnolent as the women entered the house. Hearing their voices, soft and feathery, drifting in low from the entry hall, he opened a drowsy, bloodshot eye. "I think I'll have another lie-down," he heard Trawley saying; "I'm quite tired for some reason."

"Yeah, me too," answered Freeboard. Then footsteps ascending the stairs, doors softly opening and closing. Dare's eye slid shut and he took a deep breath. And then he opened both eyes and raised his head and listened. A sound. Yes, again! A distant whine and then a yip! And then another! Dare's face was aglow with rapture.

"*Boys!*"

He had brought them after all!

He would have to go and find them.

"Dr. Case?" he called loudly.

He got up and walked over toward the Great Room.

"Doctor?"

It occurred to him he didn't know which bedroom Case had taken. He hurried to the kitchen, walked in and looked around, calling, "Morna?" But no one was there.

He breathed deeply.

He would have to go alone.

CHAPTER SEVEN

UNEASY AND CONFUSED, fatigued, her body heavy, Freeboard lay on her bed staring up at the ceiling. Something was wrong, she knew. What was it? She tightened her hands into fists at her sides, shut her eyes and attempted to shake it off. The middle finger of her hand lifted up. "Haunt *this*!" Abruptly she sat up and swung her legs off the bed. She listened. A piano being played. She smiled. Rachmaninoff's Concerto #2, the second movement, softly reflective and colored with longing. It was the only piece of classical music she could recognize, although she never had learned its name. She had heard it in a movie.

Mesmerized, Freeboard got up from the bed, walked out into the hall and leaned over the balustrade. She saw Case at the piano below. Drawn, she walked slowly down the stairs and through the Great Room, not noticing her sense of anxiety had vanished. When she'd reached the piano, Case looked up. He smiled, then looked down at the keys and stopped playing. "Oh, well, something like that," he said in self-deprecation. He shrugged.

"That's my favorite piece of music," Freeboard told him.

"Oh, really? Well, in that case I'll continue."

"Yeah, you do that."

He lifted his hands and again began to play.

Freeboard looked around her. "Where's Terry?"

"Last I saw him he was stretched out on a couch in the library posing as a very large illuminated manuscript."

"A what?"

"He'd had a number of scotches."

"Yeah, right."

"Did you and Anna enjoy your little walk?" Freeboard frowned, looking puzzled.

"What walk?" Case stared. A strange sadness had come into his eyes. He lowered his gaze and shook his head.

"Never mind."

"WHERE ARE YOU, boys? Come to me! Come!"

Apprehensive, barely breathing, grasping for courage, Dare picked his way slowly along the hallway deep within the maze of rooms within the house. The hall was interior, there were no windows, and the light from ornamental copper sconces was dim. "Boys? Come on, boys. Where are you?" Dare hiccoughed. He could taste a bit of scotch coming up. He made a face. And then froze as from somewhere behind him he again heard a small creaking sound, slow and careful, like a stealthy footfall. The sconce lights flickered and dimmed. Dare swallowed. Come along now, don't be absurd, he thought. Aloud he said, "I've written this scene a dozen times." He turned his head and peered down the length of the hall. There was nothing. The lights came back up to full brilliance and instantly the author felt the atmosphere change, like the sudden relenting of a powerful gravity, leaving the corridor buoyant and free. Dare exhaled, turned around again and slowly walked on until he arrived at a door at his left. He opened it and looked into a spacious bedroom. "Boys?" He glanced around, then closed the

door and moved on. Another door. He opened
it and looked in. Another bedroom with a four-
poster bed. To his right he saw a makeup table.
The room had belonged to a woman.

"Boys?"

No response. Yet he entered and closed
the door softly behind him. Something had
drawn him. He looked out a window at the
pale, thin light of end of day. The branches
of the oak trees were gnarled silhouettes, like
those used to illustrate a Grimm fairy tale.
Dare turned on a lamp on a bedside table
where he noticed a large, round porcelain
pillbox, white, and decorated with little
purple rabbits. He picked it up carefully and
opened it. It was a music box. It was playing.
Dare stared as the tiny chimes tinkled in the
air, a Stephen Foster tune, "Jeannie with the
Light Brown Hair." Who had wound it up?
Dare wondered. He gently closed the lid. It
was then that something else began to strike
him as odd. He reached down and rubbed a
finger along the table, then held it to his gaze
for examination. The room and its contents
were completely free of dust, and the surface
of woods appeared newly waxed. Who was
cleaning the house? Were there unseen staff
in a hidden wing? He thought of his vision,
the man in black. LSD or a *truly* silent butler?
he wondered. "Also invisible," he muttered.

Then he sniffed. He smelled perfume in the air, the scent of roses.

"Can I help you?"

Startled, Dare yelped and whirled around. Morna was staring at him, expressionless.

Her eyes flicked down to the music box.

"Are you looking for something?"

Dare said, "No," but the reply was almost soundless, gasping through the ice that had formed in his larynx. He cleared his throat with effort and amended, "I mean, yes. My dogs. Have you seen them?"

"The little ones? No."

He absently nodded. He was staring at her neck.

He looked past her and noticed that the door was still closed. He stared at her neck again. He was frowning. Then something occurred to him. "How did you know that my dogs are little?" he asked. "Have you seen them in the house? Are they here?"

Morna smiled, as if in secret amusement, then without another word she turned and glided to the door, pulled it open and exited the room. For a moment Dare stared at the open doorway, and then down at the music box still in his hand. He gently replaced it on the table, then walked out into the hall. "Morna?" he began. He had another question concerning the dogs. But in the hall he saw no one. She was gone.

He was suddenly electrified by a sound. Muted and distant. The yapping of a dog. Dare beamed and then frowned as he realized that the bark was of a larger animal. "Boys?" Then he called again, "*Men?*" The yapping continued. Dare began to move toward the sound apprehensively. At the end of the hall he saw a door and as he neared it the yapping grew louder, more excited, then elided into threatening growls and barks interlaced with piercing whines, as of fright. Near the door, Dare stopped as the voice of a man came through from behind it: "What is it, boy? What?"

So there *was* someone here, thought Dare. There was staff.

He grasped the doorknob and opened the door.

Dare gaped. He was looking at what seemed to be a kitchen.

Trembling, teeth bared, a collie dog was confronting him, alternately whining and growling and barking. At a table sat a man and a woman in their fifties and what looked to be a husky young Catholic priest dressed in cassock and surplice and purple stole, while by a window stood a taller old redheaded priest who gripped a book that was bound in a soft

red leather. The man and the woman and the younger priest were staring toward Dare as if in numb apprehension, but the redheaded priest by the window seemed calm as he walked to the table routinely, unhurriedly, to pick up a vial filled with colorless liquid. A woman in a housekeeper's uniform entered the room. She was carrying a steaming pot of coffee. As she moved toward the table she glanced toward the door, dropped the pot and emitted a piercing shriek, and as she did the old priest uncapped the vial, flicked his wrist and shot a sprinkle of its contents at the dumbfounded author, whereupon the people in the kitchen vanished.

Shaken, Dare whirled about and ran for his life.

ANNA TRAWLEY WAS dreaming that Gabriel Case had walked up to her bedside and put out his hand to her. "Come, Anna," he said to her gently. And then she was alone, carrying a candle and walking in the underground passage to the crypt. She knew that she was looking for something but she didn't know what it was. She stopped and raised the candle. The crypt was before her. She listened. A whispering voice. Dr. Case. "Anna," he was saying. "Anna Trawley." Then the huge stone door of the crypt came open and out of it floated an open coffin containing the white-shrouded figure of a person whose face was indiscernible, a blank. "Look, Anna! Look!" the voice of Case again whispered. The face in the coffin began to take form and Anna Trawley was suddenly awake.

Screaming.

CHAPTER EIGHT

CASE LIFTED AN eyebrow.

"Refresh your drink?" he asked.

"Refresh my *life*," Freeboard muttered.

Broody, quietly on edge, a little drunk, she was slouched in a stool at the library bar as she tamped out her Camel Lite in an ashtray overflowing with a smother of crushed, bent butts. Behind the counter Case picked up a fluted martini pitcher and poured into Freeboard's glass before beginning to prepare another batch.

"That's all of it," he murmured. "I'll have more in just a shake."

Freeboard woozily lifted her glass. "*Salud!*"

They had been at the bar for almost an hour. Freeboard had wanted a drink. She'd had several, and was verging on fluency in several languages theretofore unrecorded by man. In the meantime, their conversation had been casual, much of it centered on questions by Case about "your fascinating friend, Mr. Terence Dare." Now the realtor observed with fogged, droopy eyes as Case poured Bombay gin atop the ice cubes that he had just dropped into the pitcher. They made a liquidy, crackling sound.

"Doc, are you on the level?"

Case looked up at the realtor.

"Pardon?"

"I mean spookwise. You're not into this only because of the dinero or you maybe saw *Ghostbusters* twice and got jazzed?"

"I can virtually swear that number two was not the reason," Case averred. "And as far as the dinero goes, you're the only one I know who's ever paid me for this work."

Freeboard fumbled for her cigarette pack on the bar.

"How do you live?"

Case eyed her with a kindly patience.

"The university pays me," he said gently. "I teach."

"Oh, yeah yeah."

"I'm a teacher."

"Hey, I got it, okay? You want to drop it?" Freeboard glared and lit her cigarette with unsteady hands, then set her solid gold lighter on the counter with a thump.

Case lifted the pitcher and topped off her glass.

"Another olive?" he asked her politely.

"You married?"

"Yes, I am."

She looked away and muttered, "Who gives a shit?"

She picked up a book that was resting on the counter, standing it on end as she eyed its cover. *"The Denial of Death,"* she read aloud. "Is this good?"

"Yes, I think so." Case was pouring a martini for himself. "I mean to reread it tonight," he told her. "The author's Ernst Becker."

"Who's in it?"

"It isn't a movie."

She let the book drop.

Case plopped an olive in his glass and took a sip.

"Are you married, Joan?" he asked her.

She looked down, blew out cigarette smoke and shook her head.

"Never married?" he persisted.

"Never married."

"Any family?"

"All dead. I was the youngest," Freeboard said. "I'm the last."

"No other relatives?"

She looked down into her drink. "No, no one."

"Mr. Dare is rather close to you, I've noticed."

"He's the only man I know who'd never hurt me."

"Men have hurt you very often, Joan?"

Dismissively waving her hand, she said, "Ah, fuck it."

She plucked up her martini glass, sipped, and then set down the glass with a bang. Then she snatched at the book and stood it on end. "So what's this all about?" she said.

"You wouldn't like it."

Abruptly she laid the book down, staring off.

"God, I just had that déjá vu feeling again."

"Oh?"

She nodded. "Yeah. Real strong."

Case folded his arms atop the counter, leaning forward.

"Joan, I'd like to hear more about your work. Do you enjoy it?"

"Shit, I love it to pieces."

"How nice."

"I'd rather sell a fucking town house than piss."

"That should settle any lingering ambiguity in the matter."

Freeboard looked out a window. "This place is so isolated."

"Completely."

"I wonder if it's burglarized a lot."

"I don't think so," said Case without expression.

"Well, don't look at me like I'm some kind of retard," she blurted, her droopy eyes narrowing with resentment. "A lot of Navy Seals later on become criminals. Why do you think Malibu keeps getting ripped off?"

"I'd never thought of that."

"This place would be ripe."

"I see your point."

Freeboard tilted up the book again, narrowly avoiding knocking over her glass. Case grabbed it by the stem before it could fall.

"Hey, man, thanks," said Freeboard slurrily.

"Don't mention it," said Case.

"Good hands."

She looked back at the cover of the book.

"And so what's this about, Doc? Is it good?"

"Well, it deals with our terror of death," answered Case, "and how we avoid it by trying to distract ourselves with sex and money and power."

Freeboard eyed him in blank incomprehension.

"Who needs death for all that?" she said.

"Well, exactly."

She stared at the book.

"I love my life," she murmured.

"So you should," said Case. "Lots of toys."

Freeboard propped an elbow on the bar and then lowered her head into her hand. Case could no longer see her face. "Lots of toys," she said weakly. She nodded. And then, the words muffled and narrow in her throat, she murmured, "Yeah, a whole lot of toys. A whole bunch."

Case stared. "Something wrong?" he asked.

She shook her head.

"Can't you tell me?"

She was silently sobbing into her hand.

Case set down his glass and gripped her forearm very gently.

"Can't you tell me? Please tell me," he said.

"I don't know. Sometimes I cry and don't know why. I don't know. I don't know."

She continued to sob.

"What were you thinking about just now?" Case asked her.

Freeboard shook her head. "I don't know."

He touched a comforting hand to her cheek.

"Then just cry, dear," he said. "Just cry."

He looked up as a troubled Dare entered the room and sped stiffly and immediately to the bar. The author's glance quickly taking in Freeboard's demeanor, he pronounced, "I see the serious drinking flag is flying." He slid onto a stool.

"What's your pleasure, Mr. Dare?" Case inquired.

"A new body," Dare answered, "and a brain that doesn't know who I am."

"I've got martinis all mixed."

"No, no, no!" Dare pointed to the liquor bottles shelved behind Case. "Please just hand me the Chivas and a glass," he requested.

Case reached for the bottle. "You look deathly," he said. "What's the trouble?"

Case set down the bottle and looked solicitous.

"The trouble? Well, I'll tell you the trouble," snapped Dare. About to speak, he caught sudden sight of Freeboard staring at him as she dabbed at her eyes with a tissue.

Dare shut his mouth and turned away. He said, "Nothing." He picked up the bottle, poured out two fingers, put it back, and then set his glass down on the bar emphatically. "Nothing's wrong whatsoever. Not a thing."

Anna Trawley now entered the room. Visibly upset, she moved swiftly to the bar and sat beside Dare.

"Hello, Anna. Have a drink?" asked Case.

"Yes, a double," said Trawley tightly.

"Then I gather nothing's wrong," said Case.

"Beg your pardon?" she asked. "I didn't get that."

Case stared at her innocently. "Just a comment."

Dare turned to look at Trawley, examining her drawn and ashen face and then her shaking hands now clasped atop the counter. He looked back into her eyes.

"What did *you* see?" he asked her.

At this Freeboard roused herself.

She said, "What? What do you mean? Who saw what?"

"I saw nothing," said Trawley, staring fixedly ahead.

"I saw less," replied Dare.

"Well, that settles it," said Case. He pulled a bottle off the shelf.

"Dry sherry with a twist?" he asked Trawley.

She stared at him oddly.

"Why, yes," she said at last. "Exactly."

She continued to stare.

Case saw Dare gulping down two more fingers of scotch.

"Your health," said Case, looking over at the author.

"It isn't funny," growled Dare.

"I didn't say it was funny."

"It was *nothing*," Dare insisted.

"I know."

"What in freak are you all *talking* about?" demanded Freeboard. She'd been glaring back and forth, her confusion and irritation mounting. Dare patted her hand. "Never mind."

Case put the sherry in front of Trawley. "I notice you staring," he said to her quietly. "Are you getting any sense of something yet?"

"Nothing new," she said almost inaudibly.

"I didn't get that," said Case.

Her gaze bored into his eyes. "Nothing new," she repeated.

"Oh."

Case glanced at the television set. "Oh, I do wish these TVs and radios would work," he bemoaned. "I'd so love to see the six o'clock news."

"Yes, no doubt," murmured Trawley. "So would I. But I certainly don't want to see myself on it."

"What was that?" asked Case.

She said, "Nothing."

Trawley sipped at her sherry. Her hand was still trembling.

"Speaking of the news," began Case. He turned back to the bar. Dare and Freeboard, he saw, were speaking quietly together. Case cleared his throat, and said, "And now what do we think about President Clinton's handling of foreign policy?"

A sudden hush fell upon the room. Freeboard and Dare had abruptly stopped talking and mutely turned to stare at Case. Their expressions, like Trawley's, were blank and numb. Not a breath, not a thought appeared to stir in the room.

Case looked from face to face, his eyes a question.

At last Dare frowned and asked, "*Whose* handling?"

Case paused, as if waiting for something, and then answered with a tinge of what could have been regret. "Oh, I meant to say President Bush. Awfully sorry. Yes, sorry. I misspoke."

The trio continued to stare, still motionless, and then they all looked down into their drinks. Trawley took a sip of her sherry, then, and turned to look out a window at the blood-red massive ball of the sun slipping low upon the mud-brown waters of the river.

"Nearly dark," she said softly. "Night's coming."

Case didn't move. He was staring at the three of them.

He lowered his head and shook it.

IN HER ROOM LATER on Trawley opened her diary, pressed it flat, reviewed her last entry, and then carefully penned her next notation:

PAST NINE. DINNER OVER. *I continue to be frightened. And what of it? To exist in the limitless dark of this universe, bruised and unknowing whence we came and where we go, to take breath on this hurtling piece of rock in the void—these alone are a terror in themselves, are they not? Fear, if we correctly observe our situation, is our ordinary way, like feeding, like dying. And yet what I'm feeling now is quite totally different; it is a terror of another kind. Not of ghosts. There is something else here that I am sensing, something chillingly alien and implacable; I fear it even more than the world. Case wants a séance tonight. It's so perilous. God help me. I dread what might come through that door!*

CHAPTER NINE

FREEBOARD WAS SITTING on the edge of her bed and the edge of her mind when she heard the rapping. Pensive and frowning, deeply troubled, her elbows were propped atop her knees while she cupped her face between her hands. Facedown and open on the bed beside her was a copy of the book, *The Denial of Death*. She had been reading it for a time but then her eyes had begun to hurt.

Although not nearly as much as her head.

The knocking again. Two raps. Much louder.

Freeboard didn't bother looking up.

"Knock it off, will ya, Terry? Cut it out!"

She heard her door opening and looked up at Dare.

"It's me," he said tensely.

"How would *you* know?"

Dare came over to the bed and sat beside her.

"Are you sitting on my glasses, Terry?"

"No. Joan, there's something very creepy in our midst."

"Please don't start with me, Terry. I mean it."

"My dear, I'm dead earnest," said Dare. She heard a tremor in his voice and looked up. He was pale and his eyes were tight and blinking. "I haven't been as frightened since I dreamed I was a Zulu trapped in the locker room of Rudyard Kipling's club."

Freeboard searched his eyes and found genuine terror.

She frowned. "You seeing things, Terry?" she asked him.

"Joan, I swear to you, I haven't dropped acid in years!"

He raised his right hand as if taking an oath.

Freeboard pondered.

"It's got residual effects, remember? Remember the giant squids with the ray guns and the letter of reference from Cheech and Chong?"

Dare pushed up the sleeve of his shirt, disclosing a red and vivid welt running up from his inner wrist to his forearm. "Does this look as if I'm seeing things, Joanie? Take a look at this! Look at my arm!"

Freeboard stared mutely at the welt for a moment. She looked up at him quizzically and said, "How'd you do that?"

"I saw a group of people in the back of the house," explained Dare. "Two of them were priests."

"They were *what*?"

"I said *priests*!"

"Oh, for chrissakes, Terry!"

"I mean it! One of them threw something at me! *This* happened!"

Freeboard reached out her hand as if about to touch the welt.

Dare flinched. "No, don't touch it!" he exclaimed.

"Looks like a burn," she said quietly.

"It is!"

Freeboard looked up at him. She looked dubious.

"You weren't ironing your scrapbook or anything, were you? I mean, where *are* these priests?"

"I don't know," answered Dare. "They disappeared."

"They ran away?"

"They simply vanished."

Freeboard turned and rolled her eyes. "Yeah, they vanished."

Dare thrust out his arm and showed the welt. *"This didn't!"*

She stared at it soberly. "It could have happened when Morna spilled the coffee on you, Terry."

"Yes, but wouldn't I have known that?"

"Yeah, maybe."

"I've tried to call the boatman to see about getting off the island, but—"

"You turdhead! What happened to 'I am Doubt'?"

"It got mugged in the alley by 'I am burned!' Look, the boatman didn't answer." Dare's manner was earnest and pressing, urgent. "No machine, no nothing," he continued. "I tried to call a helicopter service. No answer. I tried to call Pierre about the dogs. No answer. The *service* doesn't even pick up. You remember how you asked if today was a holiday?"

"Yeah. It's like Manhattan got nuked or something."

"And have you taken a really close look at Morna?"

Freeboard stared at Dare's hands. They were resting on his thighs. "Why, Terry, your hands are shaking!" she marveled.

"All those tiny purple spots on her face and neck?"

"What do you mean?"

"Well, she has them. They're known as *petechiae*. I researched that for *Gilroy's Confession*."

"And so?"

"They're what you see when someone dies from suffocation."

Freeboard stared.

"Oh, Mr. Dare? Miss Freeboard? Are you there?"

Case. He was calling up from the Great Room and his voice had a sinister lilting quality, as if it were coming from a fog-shrouded moor. Dare and Freeboard looked at one another in surmise.

Where had it come from, this fear? How had it jelled?

"Could I speak to you a moment?" Case called up to them again.

"He sounds just like Freddy Krueger," whispered Dare.

"Oh, shut up!"

Dare got up, went out the door and stepped into the hallway. Leaning over the balustrade he looked down and saw Case standing next to a round game table where Anna Trawley already was seated. "Ah, there you are," said Case. "And Miss Freeboard? Is she there?"

"Yeah, I hear you," Freeboard called out from the room. "What's up?" The next moment the realtor appeared at the balustrade.

"What's harpooning?" she asked without a smile.

"If you'll both come down we can start."

"Start what?"

"The seance."

CHAPTER TEN

WOULD YOU SIT here beside me, Mr. Dare?" Trawley asked.

"Why beside you? Do you feel I'm more in need of vibrations?"

"Oh, for shitssakes sit down!" Freeboard told him.

Trawley patted the seat to her left. "Right here."

"Very well," agreed Dare. He sat down.

"And you here on my right, Miss Freeboard," Trawley told her. Freeboard nodded and quickly took her place. Case was already in the chair across from Trawley.

"Thank you," said the psychic. "We can start."

On top of the game table rested a Ouija board with an American-style planchette, a cream-colored, heart-shaped piece of plastic with a circular window set in its center. The room was in darkness except for the fireplace flames and the flickering light on the table from a group of thick candles arranged close by.

Trawley lifted an eyebrow at Dare. "No tape recorder?"

Dare shook his head. His manner brusque, he said, "No. No, I'll remember. No need." The author glanced up to the second-floor landing and a video camera put there by Case. It was aimed at the table. "And it's going on film," Dare noted further.

Trawley nodded. "Very well. Now then, you may have a few misconceptions that I think I should disabuse you of."

Dare murmured, "Of which I should disabuse *you*." Distracted, he was staring at the planchette and was hardly aware that he had spoken. Trawley glanced in his direction "There will not be any floating tambourines, Mr. Dare. No ectoplasm. No ghostly apparitions. No voices. Nothing will possess me or attempt to speak through me. Yet if something is here, it will show us, it will make itself known. My pitiful"—she turned to look at Case—"gift," she finished, "is somehow to focus its energies, that's the best that we can expect. We don't need to have the lights off, incidentally."

"Oh, I know that," said Case. "It's just to put us in the mood."

"Well, we're in it," snapped Dare.

Freeboard folded her arms and looked at Trawley.

"And so what's supposed to happen?" she asked.

"I don't know," said the psychic.

"You don't *know*?"

"No. Perhaps nothing at all will occur."

Trawley held out her hands to either side. "Now all join hands, would you please?"

They followed her instruction.

"I need you to be quiet and perfectly still," said Trawley. "Try to help me, please. Even if you think this is foolishness, try not to speak and keep your thoughts fixed on me." She closed her eyes. "Think only of me and what I'm trying to do," she said. "Now then, shut your eyes, please."

They obliged, and as they did, a slow creaking sound was heard, as of a shutter or a door coming slightly ajar.

Dare's eyes opened wide.

"Mr. Dare, are your eyes still open?" asked the psychic.

"How on earth did you know that, madam? Are you peeking?"

"I am not. Would you close them, please?"

"I will." Dare shut his eyes.

"And now we wait," uttered Trawley. "Try to help me. And wait. Just wait." Her final words were barely a whisper. She appeared to breathe slowly and deeply for a time. And then again she spoke. It was a quiet question: "Is there anyone here with us?"

They waited. Only the crackling of the fire could be heard.

"Is there anyone here?" the psychic repeated.

Another deep silence ensued. A minute passed.

Dare opened his eyes and was about to comment tartly when the candles and the fireplace flames were snuffed out, as if extinguished by a single massive breath. The Great Room was plunged into absolute darkness and the scent of the river was abruptly in the air. "Oh, well, really," said Dare in a voice that was straining to be blithe: "How utterly banal and degrading. I saw this scene in *The Uninvited*. Is our budget too tight for a fragrance of mimosa, or is *eau de clam chowder* the scent of the day?"

Freeboard shut her eyes, then put her head down and shook it.

From somewhere a keening sound arose, and then a violent banging that kept repeating, insistent, implacable, jarring their souls.

"Domino's Pizza," said Dare. "They're aggressive."

But his voice held the hint of a tremor.

Case stood up and moved deliberately across the room to where a wooden shutter, tossed by a gusting breeze, was crashing against the inner wall. "There's our trouble," said Case. "We may have another storm coming up."

He reached the window, locked it shut and then returned.

He struck a match to relight the thick green candles.

"Oh, can't we have the lights on?" asked Trawley.

"Yes, of course." Case snuffed out the match. He walked over to the wall and flipped a number of switches, turning on all of the sconce lights and lamps. Coming back to the table, he took his chair and remarked, "So it seems it was really Mother Nature, Mr. Dare, and not Mother Trawley who produced the cliché."

"My apologies, madam," Dare told her.

"Now then, may we proceed?" Trawley asked him.

"Your servant."

As the others closed their eyes, Dare goggled. Far across the room he saw the collie dog he believed he had seen in the other wing. It was staring through a partly open door that led to the inner maze of the house. With a yip it scampered back and out of sight.

"Mr. Dare, are your eyes closed?" Trawley asked softly.

"Oh, for God's sakes, *yes!*" Dare irritably answered. He immediately closed them. There followed a silence like that of cathedrals at dawn or in lucid dreams of flying.

"Is there anyone here?" asked Trawley quietly.

More moments passed in silence.

Dare opened his eyes and let go of the hands he'd been gripping. "I don't want to do this anymore," he said tightly.

The others at the table opened their eyes.

"Oh, well, it really doesn't seem to be working, now, does it?" said Trawley. She sounded very matter-of-fact.

"No, it seems not," answered Case. He looked at Freeboard. "Well, so far it seems your clients should be perfectly safe here, Joan."

"I didn't say that I don't sense a presence," said Trawley.

Freeboard looked away and murmured, "Shit."

Case probed Trawley's eyes. "Good or evil?"

She waited before answering: "Dangerous."

Dare made a move to get out of his chair, but Freeboard gripped him by the wrist and tugged him down.

"Let's see what happens, 'I am Doubt,'" she said firmly. "Okay?"

Dare saw the interest in her face and looked appalled.

Case shifted in his chair.

"Well, shall we try something else now, Anna? Something new?"

Trawley stared at him intently for a moment, saying nothing. Then she lowered her gaze to the table and said, "Yes. The Ouija board. Just as you suggested," she added.

Case nodded his head toward the board. "Worth a try."

Dare looked past him to the door where he'd seen the dog.

"Mr. Dare, is that agreeable?" Case asked him.

Dare shifted his glance. "Yes, what's the harm?"

"Did you see something?"

"See something?"

"I saw you looking past me rather oddly."

"No, nothing," Dare said curtly. He looked tense.

"Very well, then, let's begin," said Case. "I'll just observe, if you don't mind. Go ahead. You've all done this before?"

"I know the drill." Freeboard nodded.

"And you, Mr. Dare?"

Dare said, "No. Nor have I bungee-jumped from a bridge in Lahore with a purple sacred cow in my arms."

Trawley instructed him, and moments later all except Case were resting their fingertips on the planchette as it glided slowly around on the board.

"That's it," said Trawley. "Get the feel of it a bit."

"Of course it's *you* who'll be actually moving it," Case ruminated. "Your unconscious minds, I mean. On the other hand, I think that if there *were* something to it, it's because the unconscious must in some unknown way form a bridge to the other side: the spirit gives a message to the unconscious, which in turn prompts our fingers to move the planchette. You think that's right, Anna?"

"Possibly. Yes." The psychic nodded.

"Say again why we're doing this," Freeboard asked. She was staring intently at the planchette. Something was pulling her into this process. And somehow unnerving her as well.

"To be sure that the house is safe for your clients," said Case.

He and Trawley shared a look.

"Yeah, that's right," Freeboard grunted.

Dare shook his head and murmured, "Shameless!"

Her gaze still fixed on the roaming planchette, Freeboard murmured, "You're fucking up the spirits here, dickhead."

"Let your hands be at rest now," Trawley advised them. The planchette ceased its motion and the psychic closed her eyes. A deep silence ensued. Trawley lowered her head.

"Is there anyone here?" she asked.

Nothing happened; the planchette stayed at rest. Then as Trawley began to repeat the question, the planchette made a lurching slide to the YES in the upper left corner of the board. Dare stared at the word. "I didn't do that," he said quietly. He shifted his glance to Freeboard. "Did you move it?"

"No, *you* did."

Trawley uttered softly again:

"Who is here?"

The Great Room was still. The air was thick. And waiting.

Trawley's brow began to crease. Vaguely troubled, she again probed the darkness:

"Who is here?" she repeated. Almost before she had finished speaking, the planchette lurched downward with vigor to a letter. Trawley opened her eyes in apprehensive surmise.

"U. The letter U," noted Case.

Again the planchette began to move swiftly, carrying their fingers from letter to letter.

"Come on, Terry, you're moving it!" Freeboard accused him.

"I am not!"

Case called out the letters one by one as the planchette moved to Z, and then U, and then R - D - E - R - E - R - H - E - R - E .

And stopped.

"Zurderer here?" Dare wondered.

He was rapt and intent, all cynicism vanished.

"Makes no sense," Freeboard commented, frowning.

As she spoke, the planchette glided up to the NO.

"'No,'" said Case, looking thoughtful.

Then, "There it goes again," he said abruptly.

The planchette moved to Z and from there to M.

"Z-M," Case murmured. "'No Z-M.' What on earth could that possibly mean?" he pondered.

"Not Z but M," guessed Dare.

He looked up. "The Z is wrong; it should be M!"

"'Murderer here'!" exclaimed Freeboard. The planchette fluttered up to the YES.

"My God, it's Quandt!" Dare breathed.

A shocked hush fell upon them. Trawley lifted her eyes to Case.

"Are you Edward Quandt?" she asked the presence.

Somewhere a door creaked slightly open. Freeboard was watching it as it happened: it was the thick carved door that led down to the crypt. She turned to look at Dare as she noticed that his fingers felt icy cold, and as she did the planchette slid upward again. It stopped on the NO. Then rapidly it flew to other letters and numerals. As it did, Case called them out: "M — O — N — E — O — F — U."

Her eyes on the board, Trawley paled.

"'Murderer one of you,'" she said softly.

For a moment no one spoke. Then Freeboard erupted, "I'm getting freaked! Take your hand off it, Terry!"

"I'm not moving it," said Dare.

"*I said, take off your hand!*"

Dare caught a glimpse of Trawley and was taken aback to see tears in her eyes. Then he noticed Case staring at the psychic with compassion; he was shaking his head and seemed to be mouthing the words, "No, Anna. No. Not you." What the *hell* was this about? the author wondered. He lifted his fingers from the planchette.

"Tell us who is the person who is communicating," said Trawley in a husky, low voice. "Who are you? What is your name?"

They waited but the planchette did not move. Freeboard turned to Dare with a knowing and accusatory smile. "*Ah-huh!*" she said, nodding her head. Then abruptly she turned her head back to the board as the planchette moved rapidly under their fingers.

Case called off the letters. "A…" he began.

On the next one, Freeboard joined him, chiming in, "Ce."

Case looked up at her and smiled. Then he leaned back and watched with what looked like satisfaction as the realtor alone went on calling out the letters:

"C…E…P…" The planchette hesitated. "T."

Then the movement ceased.

"'Accept,'" said Dare with a frown. "It spells 'accept'."

"So what's *that* supposed to mean?" puzzled Freeboard. "'Accept.' Accept what?"

"Or who?" mentioned Dare.

The planchette was moving again, swinging wildly back and forth between the letters G and O.

"G—O—G—O," murmured Dare.

Trawley winced and put her head into her hand. It was as if she'd been stricken by a sudden stab of migraine. As she lifted her hand from the plastic planchette, it flew off the board and rattled onto the floor, where after brief motion it at last lay still.

Case put a hand on Trawley's arm. He looked concerned.

"What is it? What's wrong?" he asked.

"I have to stop. An awful stabbing in my head."

"Oh, I'm so sorry," said Case.

Frowning, Freeboard stared at the Ouija board. "'Go.' 'Accept,'" she wondered aloud. "What in shit could that mean?"

"What did you *mean* it to mean?" Dare said coolly.

"And what the hell does *that* mean?"

"Oh, well, clearly you were moving it, Joan."

"Bull-*shit*!"

"You're suggesting Mrs. Trawley was moving it? Bizarre!"

Freeboard stood up and strode away from the table.

"I've had it, guys. Really. Adios."

"Where are you going, love?" Dare called after her.

"I don't know," she replied. "I don't care."

She was headed for the foyer.

"Maybe for a walk," she called back. "I need air."

The clacking of her heels on the floor receded. The front door opened and closed. She was gone. Case turned back to Trawley. She had both elbows propped on the table now, her head cradled down into her hands.

"How's the head?" Case asked with concern.

"Getting better."

Dare's glance shifted back and forth between them.

"Are we finished?" he asked stiffly.

"Yes, I think so," said Case.

Dare stood up and addressed them both. "Let me thank you for these thoroughly exhilarating moments. Never have I felt quite so glad to be alive since Evel Knievel invited me to join him in leaping a chasm in Ulan Bator. You'll excuse me? I'm finding that I need to make a call." The author turned on his heel and strode toward the staircase.

Case watched his quick footsteps ascending the steps, saw him walk down the hall and disappear into his room.

Case dropped his glance to Trawley.

"Shall I ask Morna to bring you some aspirin?"

Trawley said, "No." It was barely audible.

"Been a bit of a bust tonight, hasn't it?" said Case.

Trawley nodded her head. Case thoughtfully appraised her in silence for a time and then he reached out his hand and touched it to her arm.

"Did you move the planchette?" he asked her quietly.

She dropped her arms to the table, lifted her head and stared at him blankly. "What?"

"I mean, unconsciously," he said to her gently. "Do you think you caused your daughter Bethie's death? That you're the murderer?"

Her look was incredulous.

"I really don't know what to say," she responded.

"When your daughter Bethie died—" Case began.

But she cut him off.

"I never told you that my daughter's name was Bethie."

HEAD DOWN, HANDS deep in the pockets of her jeans, Freeboard trudged along the shoreline, lost in thought. There was an aching and a churning deep inside her, a sense of displacement, of loss, of fear, and of an answer that kept voicelessly shouting its name. *Case. That freaking Case and his freaking martinis.* That's what had started it, she brooded. *And then reading that goddam freaking book.*

Abruptly she stopped in her tracks and looked up.

Something was wrong, she felt. What was it?

The silence, she suddenly realized. No sounds. Not of the river nor of birds nor any life. She could hear herself breathing, hear the beat of her pulse.

This is weird!

Freeboard looked toward the village on the opposite shore. There wasn't any fog and the night was clear. Shouldn't there be lights? she wondered dimly. When she turned her gaze south toward Manhattan she blinked. And then suddenly her eyes were wide. She gaped numbly. She took a step backward, bewildered, frightened, and then cried out in outraged incredulity, "*What?*"

She turned and ran back toward the house.

CHAPTER ELEVEN

Breathless, Freeboard burst into the entry hall, closed the door with a bang and fell against it. She looked up at a sconce and then into the Great Room as all the mansion's lights began to flicker down to dimness. "Terry?" she called quietly. She waited. No response. Cautiously she moved into the Great Room. "Terry?" she called out more loudly.

She glanced all around.

"Dr. Case? Anna?"

The silence grew stranger. Nothing moved. Freeboard walked to the library, scanned it quickly, and then rapidly moved to behind the bar, where she poured a few fingers of rye into a glass, gulped it, and then stood there, trying to collect herself. Then her eyes grew wide and she froze as she heard a sound like rusted hinges, and then of heavy stone grinding slowly over stone. It seemed to be coming from beneath her. Freeboard darted a numb look into the Great Room and the door beneath the staircase leading to the crypt.

Shit!

It was still unlocked and ajar.

Freeboard set down her glass and strode out of the library, calling out, "Terry? Terry, where the fuck are you?"

She looked up at the door to his room.

"You up there? Terry? Dr. Case?"

She went to the stairs and quickly ascended them and then walked to the door of Dare's room. She knocked and called, "Terry?" but immediately burst into the room without waiting for an answer.

Dare was packing a suitcase that lay on the bed.

"Do come in," he said tartly. He didn't look up.

Freeboard flung the door loudly shut behind her.

"I'm beginning to think that you're right!" she said tremulously.

She swooped to the bed, sat down and watched him arranging a shirt in the bag. "I'm beginning to think there *are* ghosts," she admitted. Dare threw his hands into the air and quickly turned to her, squalling, "But I don't *want* to be right about that!"

"I'm getting freaked, Terry. Really."

Freeboard held up her hands to her own inspection.

"Look at this! I mean, *look* at this! *My* hands are shaking!"

Dare looked down and saw the trembling, then said softly, "Oh, my dear!" He dropped the lid on the suitcase and sat down beside her. Taking hold of her hands, he tightly clasped them in his own.

"Why, my dear, dear Joan," he said to her worriedly.

He looked into her eyes.

"Yes, you truly are frightened. Terribly."

She glanced at the telephone receiver; it was lying on its side on a bedstand. She could hear the dull ringing at the other end.

"Is that the boat you're calling, Terry?"

"Trying. Tell me, precious, what has happened? Tell me all."

"Take a look out the window."

"There aren't any."

"Right. Holy shit, Terry!"

"What, Joan? What is it?"

She bent and put a hand to her chest, as if trying to catch her breath. "I went outside," she told him haltingly. "The sky's clear, there's a moon, big stars. But there isn't any city there, Terry; there's no skyline of Manhattan—no lights, no planes, no nothing!" She looked up into his eyes. "God, I'm really getting scared, Terry. What's going on with this place? I wish—"

She halted. Something was different. Her glance flicked over to the telephone receiver. Dare said, "What?" Then he followed her gaze.

"The ringing," said Freeboard. "It stopped."

The silence that had settled on the room was profound. It spoke of finality, of a chapter that was ending. And a new one, something alien, about to begin. Dare stood up, reached over, picked up the receiver and slowly put it up to his ear. Then he quietly placed it back down on its cradle.

"It's dead," he said dully.

The next moment the lights in the room dimmed down and from somewhere in the house came a jarring sound, like the muffled blow of a giant sledgehammer wrapped in velvet striking a wall. Freeboard turned a frozen look to Dare. "Terry?" He sat down beside her as another blow came, and then another and another, growing louder, coming closer to the room.

"God, what is it, Terry? What?"

"I don't know."

Freeboard gasped. Her eyes widened.

"It's coming up the steps!"

"Is the door locked?"

She shook her head and said, "No! It doesn't lock!"

"Oh, my Christ!" uttered Dare.

Freeboard clutched him with both her arms.

"Jesus, Terry, hold on to me! Hold me! I'm scared!"

He glimpsed the child's fear in her eyes, the helplessness. He took hold of her and held her tightly. "Don't be frightened," he said into her ear. "It's all right!" And she might have believed it had she not felt the furious racing of his heart.

They gaped at the door.

The poundings were picking up speed, throbbing closer.

"It's out in the hall!" whimpered Freeboard. "It's coming!"

"Shh, shh, Joanie!" Dare hissed in her ear. "It may not know that we're in here! Don't move!" he ordered. "Don't make a sound!"

Dare thought of every ghost story ever written, of every imaginable malevolence conceived by every fantasist who ever had lived. Malevolence? No, that wasn't what he felt was coming toward them; it was hatred, an implacable, terrifying fury.

Her eyes wide with fright, Freeboard gasped.

"Oh, my Christ!"

The poundings had stopped in front of the door.

God in heaven! thought Dare. Let me faint! Please let me faint!

A flow of cold energy, sickening, enraged, flowed into the room in sheets, in waves. Then the presence, the stillness, at the door grew thicker. Moments later there were tiny creaking sounds, tiny thumps, like fingers feeling at the doorframe, as if they were seeking an entry point. Freeboard jammed a knuckle of her hand into her mouth in an effort to stifle another whimper. There were tears in her eyes. Then the probings ceased and from the hall they heard only a threatening silence. And then they were gasping, crying aloud, at a deafening crash against the door. And then another and another, relentless, unceasing, a battering ram made of murderous thoughts.

"Dr. Caaaaase!"

It was Freeboard. Terrified. Shrieking.

Abruptly the pummeling came to an end and Freeboard's cry bled into silence and the frigid and weightless air of the room. Dare felt her trembling uncontrollably. "It's all right!"

he whispered in her ear, then put a comforting hand against her cheek. *What's the meaning of this ludicrous courage?* he marveled. It would never have occurred to him the answer was love. He listened. A sound. A faint squeaking of metal. He looked and then gasped: the doorknob was turning! Dare quickly put his hand over Freeboard's eyes and tried to remember the Act of Contrition. Then the turning stopped and reversed itself, easing back to its original position. The next instant the poundings resumed, but more softly, the hammerings more muffled and pneumatic. Throbbing like a heartbeat, they were moving away, growing fainter and fainter, more distant. Dare exhaled in relief and took his hand from Freeboard's eyes. They were wide.

"What's happening?" she whispered in terror.

"It's going away," he whispered back.

And then suddenly the pounding started up in full force again, deafening, returning to the door with savage fury. Freeboard gaped and her lips were moving but her words were completely inaudible as a strident keening filled the hall and the door began to buckle and bow in its center, bulging and creaking and straining inward as if bent by an angry and unthinkable energy furiously attempting to break into the room. Freeboard's mouth was wide in a scream of terror that not even Dare was able to hear. And then he was gaping at something, astounded, for though the door was still closed he could see two figures who were standing in the hall directly in front of it as if they were about to enter: motionless and silent, staring into the room, they were the priests he thought he'd seen in the other wing. The taller one, older, with a freckled face, held a book that was bound in bright red leather. With the vision the poundings grew faster, more violent; then abruptly the energy seemed to relent and it ebbed to a muffled, steady pulsing as the door creaked back to its original shape. Freeboard cupped a hand to her mouth and emitted a stifled sob. The soft poundings receded, moving slowly down the hall, growing fainter and fainter until at last they were gone.

Freeboard took the hand from her mouth. "Jesus, Terry, I want to get out of this place!" she whispered hoarsely.

"Me too."

"You think it's gone?"

Dare shook his head. "I don't know."

He started to get up to go to the door but the realtor quickly tugged him back down. "No! Don't open it yet! I don't trust it!"

"Yes, you're right," he whispered back.

They waited. And then voices. From below. Trawley and Case.

Dare and Freeboard leaped up and moved swiftly to the door, opened it and rushed out into the hallway. Below them, Case and Trawley were ambling into the Great Room, quietly chatting. Trawley laughed. Freeboard called down to them loudly, "Hey!"

Case and Trawley looked up. Dare and Freeboard were hustling down the stairs, rushing up to them. "My God, am I glad to see you guys!" exclaimed Freeboard. She was breathless. "Where in freak have you been?" she exclaimed.

"Why, I was just showing Anna the rest of the house," replied Case. "Is something wrong? Have you seen something? Tell me." He fumbled at his pockets, as if searching for a notepad and pen. He examined their faces. "Yes, I see something's happened," he said.

"No shit! Listen, don't ever leave us like that!" Freeboard told him.

"You're so pale, dear," the psychic observed. "And you too, Mr. Dare."

"I'm in tatters," Dare declared. "Undone."

"Well, what was it?" asked Case. "What did you see?"

"I don't know," Freeboard answered. With a knuckle, she brushed away a tear from her eye. "There was something. It came down the hall. It was trying to get in, it almost bent in the door!"

"What door?" asked Case.

"To my room," said Dare.

"First we heard this loud sound," recounted Freeboard. "Like a sledgehammer pounding on the walls. The whole house shook, it filled up your brain! And then it—"

"Excuse me," said Case, looking past her. "Oh, Morna, dear?"

Dare and Freeboard turned and saw the housekeeper standing close by. Where had she come from? wondered Dare.

Morna's eyes were on Case as she answered, "Yes?"

"Have you been in the house this past hour?"

"Of course."

"Then you heard it," said Freeboard.

"Heard what, Miss?"

"Heard *what*?" Freeboard giggled.

"You heard nothing unusual, Morna?" Case asked. He was frowning and seemed dubious and uncertain.

"No, nothing at all," Morna answered serenely.

"It was shaking the *house*!" Freeboard blurted incredulously.

"Yes, *exactly*!" added Dare. "It was deafening!"

Morna gently shook her head and said softly, "I heard nothing."

"Oh, well, shit!" muttered Freeboard. "So I'm Looney Toons."

"But *I* heard it *too*," Dare exploded.

"Tell me, Morna, where were you?" Case asked, his frown deeper. "I mean, just this past hour," he added.

"In the kitchen."

"This is crazy!" blurted Freeboard. She threw up her arms.

"Will there be something further?" asked Morna.

"You're very sure, Morna?" Case persisted.

"I am. Is that all, please? I can go?"

Case held her gaze with some mysterious emotion in his eyes. It was something like longing. Or grief. Then after moments he said softly, "You may go. And thank you. Thank you more than I can say."

"Yeah, me too. Thanks a bunch," grumbled Freeboard.

"Then good night," Morna told them. She held Case's gaze for another long moment, and then turned and glided slowly toward the hall at the end of the room, the one from which she first had appeared. Freeboard watched her, nonplussed. "Good *night*?"

"There's no question of what we saw and heard," averred Dare. "Oh, well, *heard,* at least."

"You saw something?" Case raised an eyebrow.

"No, not really." Dare backed off it. "I'm afraid I misspoke."

"Oh, well, screw it. Doc, I want to get out of here," said Freeboard. "Like tomorrow. First thing. If it means I have to *swim* back, I'm outta here. Really!"

"Yes, ditto, as Joe Pendleton would say," agreed Dare.

Case looked puzzled. "Joe Pendleton?"

"The boxer in *Here Comes Mr. Jordan*," Dare told him.

"Ditto ditto," said Freeboard. "I want out."

"Yes, of course," replied Case. He seemed thoughtful, staring down at the floor as in an absent gesture he gently stroked and tugged at his lips. He shook his head. "In the meantime, we seem to have a mystery on our hands. But I think that perhaps we can solve it."

"How's that?" demanded Dare.

Case gestured toward the second-floor hallway.

"There's a camera been running up there through the séance, and another at the end of the hall. If there was anything there, it would appear on the film or on the sound track, in which case we'll have learned what we set out to find and Mr. Dare can write a mesmerizing article about it. On the other hand, if nothing turns up on the film—no hammering sounds, no ghosts…" Case shrugged and let it trail off. Then he turned to look at Freeboard.

"Would that ease your mind?" he asked.

Freeboard set her jaw firmly. "It's there."

"NOTE THE TIME code at the bottom right corner of the screen," said Case. He pointed to the spot with his finger. "As you see it reads 11:33 p.m."

He was standing by the library television set and on the screen was a view of the empty Great Room. Trawley, Dare and Freeboard watched from a sofa close to the warmth of the fireplace flames. "As you can see," continued Case, "there's nothing there. Nothing visible. No sound of any kind. No poundings. Neither camera turned up anything at all."

Dare looked flummoxed.

"Oh, well, the microphones must have malfunctioned."

"No, they didn't," said Case. "Not this one, at least. Here, watch."

Within moments Case and Trawley appeared on the monitor screen as they entered the Great Room from a hall. Their footsteps, their quiet conversation, were fully and crisply audible.

Freeboard stared at the screen and shook her head.

"That's just plain crazy," she murmured. "It's nuts."

"But no poundings and no ghosts," reminded Case.

"But I tell you we heard it!" Dare fumed. "There's no question, it was absolutely there!" His cheeks had reddened.

"Yes, it's certainly a puzzle," Case agreed. "No doubt of that." Working buttons on the video camera he'd connected to the television monitor, he was rapidly rewinding the tape. "But now here's an even deeper one," he told them. He was shaking his head. "I just don't understand it," he said. "Not at all." Then at last he said, "There. There's the spot. Now look at this. It's from when we did the séance." Case touched a little button and the tape ran forward. Once again the Great Room was projected on the screen. Near its center was the game table, with the Ouija board resting atop it.

The time code read 10:30 p.m.

Freeboard gaped. "Hey, where are we? What's going on?"

The planchette atop the Ouija board was in motion, desultorily gliding from letter to letter. But no one was seated at the table. There was no one to be seen in the room, in fact, except, for a moment, a large collie dog that appeared at the entrance to a hallway and then hastily scurried away and out of view. Dare stared at the screen, his face blanching, and Trawley was mutely shaking her head. "The date's wrong," the psychic murmured. She was staring at the date just below the time code. "It says 1998."

"We're not on the film," said Freeboard dully.

She was staring at the screen, uncomprehending and lost.

Dare leaped to his feet. "Oh, well, for godsakes, this is ludicrous! Really! It's mad! It's clearly some sort of absurd mistake!" He looked over at Freeboard. The realtor had jumped up with a wince of pain and began to move quickly away from the fireplace.

"Holy shit, I'm burning up!" she grimaced.

And then Trawley leaped up, and then Dare. "Where's this godawful heat coming from?" he complained. He followed

Freeboard and Trawley into the Great Room. Of them all, only Case seemed completely unaffected. He came to the library door and watched calmly, although not without a look of great interest and concern.

"Dear God!" Trawley cried.

With a look of surprise, she staggered backward a step, as if shoved by an invisible assailant. And then surprise was transmuted into gaping fear as she staggered yet another step back, and then another. "Someone's pushing me!" she gasped. Another shove. "Oh, my God!" she started crying; "Oh, my God!"

And now the sound of a blow against the mansion's outer wall.

"Oh, my Christ!" breathed Dare in terror. "Oh, my Christ!"

"I'm burning up, Terry!" cried Freeboard. "I'm burning!"

The pounding at the outer walls continued, thunderous, painful, penetrating bone. Lamps and tables began tipping over, scraping, sliding, hurtling through the room while huge paintings were ripped by a force from the walls and sent flying, spinning through the air of the Great Room as agony and madness descended upon it, on the house, on their bewildered, burning souls.

"Someone tell me what's happening!" Freeboard screamed, hands pressed against her ears and the torment of the poundings, and suddenly Trawley was shrieking in pain as a bloodless furrow slashed down her cheek, as if plowed by an invisible white-hot prong. A ritual chanting in Latin began, nightmarish, reverberant, and low, as if murmured by a hundred hostile voices, and then Freeboard was lifted by an unseen force and sent hurtling, shrieking, across the room to slam into a wall with a sickening final thud and crunch of shattered bone. Dare and Trawley couldn't see anymore, all their blood had rushed up into their brains as now they too were seized by the force and carried up swiftly, spinning, toward the ceiling, spread-eagled, eyes bulging in terror, screaming, until they had slammed into the mansion roof and then plunged to the floor like crumpled hopes.

It was not a dream. It was real.

PART THREE:
DÉJÀ VU

CHAPTER TWELVE

THE CARVED FRONT door of the mansion burst open as if by the force of a desperate thought. "Holy shit, is this a hurricane or what!" exclaimed Freeboard. Sopping in a glistening yellow sou'wester, she staggered and tumbled into the entry hall with a keening wind at her back. She turned to see Dare rushing up the front stoop, and Trawley, carrying a bag, behind him, slower, deliberate and unhurried. A rain of all the waters of the earth was pelting down.

Freeboard cupped a hand to her mouth:

"You okay, Mrs. Trawley?" she squalled.

"Oh, yes, dear!" the psychic called back. "I'm fine!"

A booming thunder gripped the sky by the shoulders and shook it. Dare entered and dropped a light bag to the floor. "Joan, I owe you a flogging for this," he complained. "I knew that I never should have done it."

"Well, you did it," Freeboard told him. "Now for shitssakes, watch your mouth, would you, Terry? I had to practically beg these two people to do this."

She removed her yellow windjammer hat and then gestured to the open door, where the psychic seemed to falter as she climbed the front steps. "Terry, give Mrs. Trawley a hand," ordered Freeboard. Dare snailed toward the psychic unhurriedly and reached for her bag with a drooping hand. "May I help you?"

"Oh, no thank you. I'm fine. I travel light."

"Yes, of course. Tambourines weigh almost nothing."

"*Jesus,* Terry!"

Trawley entered, took off her hat and set down her bag. "That's all right," she told Freeboard with a smile; "I didn't hear it."

Freeboard leaned into the wind and shut the door. In the silence, it was Dare who first noticed the music. "Dearest God, am I in heaven?" he exclaimed. "Cole Porter!" The author's face was alight with a child's pure bliss as from behind the stout doors that led into the Great Room drifted a melody played on a piano.

Dare stared. "My favorite: 'Night and Day'!"

Freeboard moved toward the doors.

"That you in there, Doc?" she called out.

"Miss Freeboard?"

The voice from within was deep and pleasant and oddly unmuffled by the thickness of the doors. Freeboard opened them wide and stepped into the Great Room. All of its lamps were lit and glowing, splashing the wood-paneled walls with life, and in the crackle of the firepit flames leapt cheerily, blithe to the longing in the strains of "Night and Day." Freeboard breathed in the scent of burning pine from the fire. The sounds of the storm were distant.

"Yeah, we're here!" she called out. She smiled, moving toward the piano, while at the same time removing her dripping sou'wester. Behind her came Dare and, more slowly, Anna Trawley. Freeboard's boots made a squishing sound. They were soaked.

"Ah, yes, there you all are again, safe and sound," said Gabriel Case. "I'm so glad. I was worried."

He had strong good looks, Freeboard noticed. The firelight flickered and danced on his eyes. She saw that they were dark but wasn't sure of their color.

"This storm is amazing, don't you think?" he exclaimed. "Did you order this weather, Mr. Dare?"

"I ordered Chivas."

Dare and Freeboard had arrived at the piano and stopped. Anna Trawley hung back beside a grouping of furniture that was clustered around the fireplace. She was glancing all around the room with a vaguely uncertain and tentative air.

"Are you a ghost?" said Dare to Case.

Freeboard turned to him, incredulous, her eyes flaring.

"What crap is this?" she hissed in a seething undertone.

"That's how they show them on the spook ride at Disneyland," said Dare, not lowering his voice: "a lot of spirits dancing while a big one plays piano."

Abruptly Freeboard put a hand to her forehead. "This has happened before," she said, frowning.

Case raised an eyebrow. "What was that?"

"I'm having déjà vu," Freeboard answered, troubled.

"This is neither the time nor the place," snapped Dare.

Freeboard put her hand down and looked at him oddly.

"Jesus, Terry. I knew you were going to say that."

"How could you?"

"And I knew what Dr. Case was going to say."

"That's incredible," said Case. He lifted his hands from the keyboard. "Déjà vu reflects backward, not forward," he said. He turned his head slightly and looked past Freeboard. "Ah, here—"

"Comes Morna."

Dare and Freeboard had said it together with Case.

Case stared. He glanced to Morna for a moment—she was standing close by—and then stood up, looking mildly puzzled.

"How on earth could you have known Morna's name?"

"I don't know," said Dare. He looked perplexed.

"It's all happened before."

At the quiet voice, they all turned and saw Trawley in a chair by the fireplace. Her haunted stare was on Case.

"You too?" Dare asked her.

The psychic turned to him and nodded. "Yes."

Freeboard lowered her head into a hand.

"Hey, wait a minute, guys. I'm getting weirded out."

"Yes, it truly is amazing," said Case. "Awfully strange." He continued to stand behind the piano, but his arms were now folded across his chest. He seemed somehow not a part of the group, but an observer, detached, as if watching the unfolding of a play.

Freeboard put a hand to her head, walked sluggishly over to a sofa and sat on the back of it. "I've got to sit down," she said weakly. "I'm feeling so tired all of a sudden."

"Now that you mention it," said Dare, "ditto." He headed for the furniture grouping. "What is it?" he wondered aloud. "I feel utterly drained for some reason. And I'm feeling disconnected from things."

Freeboard nodded. "Yeah, me too," she said softly.

Dare sat down on the sofa behind her.

"What is it, Joanie? What could it be?"

"I don't know." Abruptly Freeboard winced, as in pain. "Jesus-peezus, my head!" she complained.

"Is this house playing tricks with us already, Dr. Case?" Dare asked. "I mean, presuming there are tricks to be played."

Inscrutable, Case glanced over at Trawley and asked, "What's your read on all this,

Anna? What do you think? Are you having the same reaction?"

Trawley nodded.

Case unfolded his arms and scratched his head.

"Well, this is all too bizarre," he said.

"You mean it's creepy," said Freeboard.

"It's so hard to accept that you knew Morna's name," pondered Case.

Dare looked up. "What did you say?"

"Accept."

And now Freeboard was staring at Case intently, her eyes growing wide with some jarring realization.

"Accept," Dare murmured to himself.

The quiet word was affecting him strangely. Why?

"Just so baffling," said Case: "Three people with the same déjà vu; with jamais vu, in fact."

Freeboard rose from the back of the sofa, perplexity and nascent alarm in her eyes. "Hey, wait a second! What the fuck is going on here?" she demanded. Her tone was belligerent and angry.

"Yes, we're trying to figure that out," Case said blandly.

Freeboard strode up to him, stopped and examined his face.

"You're not Gabriel Case!" she declared.

Dare turned to her, taken aback.

"What on earth are you saying, Joanie?"

"I'm saying this guy is a fake! He's not Case!"

Dare looked at Case and became more confused, for he read his expression as fond, perhaps pitying.

"Are you bleeding mad, Joan?" he exclaimed.

Freeboard whirled on him.

"Terry, I've seen pictures of the man! I've talked to him!"

"Then why didn't you say so in the first place?"

"Who gives a shit, Terry! Who cares! All I know is, this man isn't Dr. Case!"

"Yes, it is!" insisted Dare.

"It is not!"

"It is! He looks *exactly* the same as every other time before: the same scar, the same—!"

The author abruptly broke off as the meaning of his words began to register upon him. "What on earth?" he whispered, shaken.

"Terry, what is it?" asked Freeboard tremulously.

She'd seen the look on Dare's face and felt a dread.

"What in God's name is happening to us?" breathed Trawley.

Stunned, Dare slowly stood up.

"This keeps happening again and again," he said numbly.

Freeboard walked over to Dare, her face ashen.

"What is it? What's wrong with us, Terry? *Tell* me!"

But the author was staring at Case, transfixed.

"Who are you?" he asked him in a weak, dead voice.

Freeboard and Trawley turned their heads to look at Case.

"Yes, who are you?" the psychic repeated dully.

Case scrutinized each of their faces intently. "Come with me," he said gravely. "I have something to show you. I think that perhaps you're now ready. Will you come? We'll just go for a pleasant little walk on the beach."

The trio stood motionless and silent. Something submissive had entered their beings. Their eyes and their postures had changed. They looked crumpled.

Case turned a kindly look to Freeboard.

"You seem tired, Joan," he said to her gently. "Are you tired?"

She shook her head mutely.

"Then come," said Case. "Let's go."

Staring and moving as if in a reverie, the trio followed Case outside. It was dawn but a heavy fog enshrouded them. Another storm was on the way: swift gray clouds scudded low above the river, and far to the north they could see dim lightning flashes, brief bright souls in the dark. Case escorted them in silence through the grove of oaks and to the path along the river where Trawley and Freeboard once ventured but then mysteriously had stopped. And now, as they neared the sharp bend in the shoreline, it was Dare who first halted, staring quietly ahead. The others stopped with him, uncertain, apprehensive. A gusting breeze ruffled Trawley's dress.

"Do you wish to continue?" Case asked softly.

No one answered. No one moved. Then at last it was Freeboard who broke away from them and strode toward the curve in the shoreline. One by one, then, slightly faltering, the psychic and the author followed. Apprehensive but satisfied, Case stayed behind. He looked to his right. Then he walked to a marshy, reeded area, where he parted a clump of brush and stared sadly at the tiny, sun-bleached skeletons of what appeared to have been two dogs. He looked up at a sound from around the bend. A horrified shriek. Freeboard. Case sighed and looked regretful, shaking his head. He hastened to catch up with the others.

Around the bend Anna Trawley had fainted. Their eyes wet with tears, Dare and Freeboard helped her up, and then together, legs trembling, they walked toward the shore where they stood and stared mutely at the rusted wreckage of a capsized motor launch whose name, though blistered and faded, could be read: *Far Traveler.*

A tiny sob escaped Trawley.

"We're all dead," said Freeboard numbly.

Dare nodded his head, looking dazed.

He said, "We died in the storm coming over."

"That's correct."

They turned and saw Case coming toward them. When a few yards away, he stopped and surveyed them, and then said to them:

"*You* were the ghosts haunting Elsewhere."

With a whimper, Trawley slumped and fell back against the wreckage. Dare reached out a trembling hand to Freeboard.

"Hold my hand, love," he said, his voice quavering slightly.

Freeboard took his hand and gripped it firmly.

"It's okay. I'm with you, Terry," she said.

"And I with you."

Case appraised them for a moment, then spoke. "I never quite completed my history of the house," he began. "I don't suppose you'd like to hear it."

"Oh, now, stop that," snapped Dare, recovering. "Bad enough to be dead without having to stand in the damp and hear tired old rhetorical devices. Could we simply go on with it, please?"

Case smiled. "For the longest time—years after their death—Edward and Riga Quandt haunted the mansion, frightening and unbalancing the tenants, even killing a few, by the force of their hatred and rage at one another. But by the middle of the eighties they had made their peace, accepted their deaths and decided to move on. But then four years ago, *you* came. You and the launch captain died coming over. The captain moved on. You three didn't. Or, to be more precise—you *wouldn't*; you refused to accept that you were dead."

"Yes, I know that now," Dare sighed. "I understand. I see everything clearly now. Very clearly."

"In that case you can explain why you refused to accept your death," Case challenged. "Can you do that, Mr. Dare?"

"Yes, of course. I was terrified that death meant damnation."

Case nodded. "Quite so. And you, Anna? Can you see what held you back?"

"Only dimly, I'm afraid."

"You'd grown addicted to your grief for your daughter."

"Oh, dear God!"

"Strange attachments that we make, don't you think?" Trawley shook her head. "Could that really be so?"

"Am I some kind of orphan here?" Freeboard said testily.

"Oh, Joan," said Case.

"Oh, yeah, 'Joan.' Cheezus-peezus," she grumbled.

"You were terrified of dying," Case told her.

"Shit, so's everyone. Come on, now. What else?"

"You couldn't bear to let go of your toys," Case said gently.

Dare turned to her loftily and sniffed, "So immature."

Freeboard glared.

"And what now?" Trawley asked. "Do we leave here?"

"That's entirely up to you," replied Case. "You may choose to cross over or choose to stay. In the meantime, my assignment here is mercifully finished."

Freeboard wrinkled up her nose. "Your assignment?"

"Yes, Morna and I—we were sent here to lead you to discover the truth. Each time in the past that you almost confronted it, you'd reject it and then start the whole cycle all over, reliving again and again your first arrival here at the mansion; all but the shipwreck, of course; you blocked that out, just like everything else that would bare your delusion. That's why you had no memory of your walk on the beach, Joan, because you knew around the next bend was *Far Traveler.* Incidentally, you've been acting out this fantasy for years, dear hearts, even *after* we arrived here to help. Stubborn sorts!"

Trawley gasped and put a hand to her cheek.

"And so that's why you seemed so familiar to me."

"Yes."

Trawley sighed. "So it was not another lifetime."

"No, Anna," said Case.

"I'm crushed."

Dare turned to Freeboard and spoke to her quietly. "Isn't it hysterical? You couldn't sell the house because you were haunting it." Freeboard lowered her head into a hand. "Honest to God, if you weren't dead already..." she murmured.

"Speaking of which," spoke up Trawley. "We were eating and drinking and all that sort of thing. Have we got new bodies?"

"Heavens no," replied Case. "It's all an illusion, my dear, nothing more. You've all been creating your own reality. The island and the mansion are solid, they are here, but you've all reconstructed them to fit your delusion."

"We're not solid?" the psychic persisted.

"You are not."

"Not even astral sort of somethings or other?"

"Give it up," Dare advised her.

"Get a life," added Freeboard in an undertone.

Dare turned to her and nodded approbation.

Case lifted his chin. "Now then, what have you decided?" he asked. "I must say, if nothing else, I do hope that if you cling to the earth you'll at least have some pity on those poor, abused people who've been trying for so long to live peacefully at Elsewhere. You know; Paul Quandt and his family, poor darlings. You've given them a devil of a time. No pun intended."

"What on earth do you mean?" asked Dare.

"You had them terrified out of their wits! You remember all that burning and flinging about and those nightmarish poundings that so frightened you all? Don't you know what was causing all that?"

"I can hardly wait to hear," Dare said dryly.

"The Quandts brought in *Jesuit priests to drive you out!*"

The author turned to Freeboard with a smirk of satisfaction.

"Did you hear that?"

"Oh, be quiet, Terry."

"Priests!"

"Shut—*up*!"

They heard someone clear his throat. It was Case.

"And so what's it to be?" he asked. "A change of frequency? I certainly hope so. I must say, I've grown fond of you all. Very fond."

Freeboard looked down and shook her head, uncertain.

"Boy, I really don't know," she said.

Case looked at her with fondness.

"I must say, I would miss you, Joan."

She looked up in surprise and said, "*Me?*"

"There'd be no more loneliness there. No more tears."

Freeboard's eyes began to fill.

"That's the deal?" she asked.

"That's the deal."

"This world was never meant to be a home to us, Joan," said Case. "This world is a one-night stand."

Abruptly Freeboard's eyes lit up in surmise. "Hey, it's you! You're the angel in my dream! Gabriel! 'The clams aren't safe'; that meant the river!"

"Well, I know what *I'm* doing," said Dare.

Freeboard turned to him and lifted an eyebrow. "You're going?"

"Yes!" exclaimed Dare. "I'm off!" The author threw a kiss in the direction of the river. "*Adieu,* space-time!" he called out. "Be good!"

He was beginning to disappear.

"Hey, wait for me!" Freeboard shouted.

She, too, was beginning to vanish.

"*Adieu,* sucky speed-reading critics and reviewers!"

Dare was almost invisible.

"Hey, slow down a second, will you?" Freeboard nattered.

"Oh, well, of course, I'm at a *much* higher frequency, Joanie."

The next moment they were gone. But a raucous cry of pique and frustration was heard, then a slap, and then the voice of Dare complaining: "No hitting in the afterlife, Joanie!"

Case and Trawley remained, and they looked at one another and smiled as they heard a dim yapping, as of two little dogs.

"Oh, my heart! Can it be?" came a waning cry from Dare.

And then Freeboard. "Can you puke in the afterlife?"

"*Boys!*"

Dare's voice, intermingled with the dogs' faint yapping, held a joy that he'd never felt or known.

In this life.

The sounds faded away.

"Well, Anna, and what about you?" Case asked her. "Are you coming? Bethie's waiting, you know."

Trawley frowned. "What's become of Dr. Case?" she asked. "I mean, the real one. Did you off him or something?"

"No, Anna. Dr. Case is alive, poor soul. When he heard that you three had died, he simply left and went back to his teaching."

"Oh."

Case took a step toward her. "Now then, shall we go together?"

Trawley stuck her hand out in front of her, halting him.

"No, not yet," she said. "First I want to know who you are."

"Would you believe that I'm a being of light?"

"Try again."

"Now *I'm* crushed," Case replied. "What's the difference *who* I am?"

"A very large one. Knowing where you came from might give me some clue as to where you might take me, if you get my drift. In this circumstance, I'd have to say that character matters."

"There isn't any smoke or mirrors, Anna. You can trust me."

"It's the smoke part that worries me," she said.

"You're not serious, Anna. Oh, come, now!"

"Well, you're certainly not an angel, now, are you? You deceived us. You pretended to be Gabriel Case."

"But of course. It's as you said, Anna— 'Dead people lie.'"

He smiled that brilliant archangel smile.

Trawley's laugh was full and rich, free of burden, overflowing. Case started forward, his arms held out to her. "And now shall we go elsewhere, my lovely?" She jabbed a fist high into the air and cried, "*Yes!*" Then rushed forward to meet him with open arms.

EPILOGUE:
1997

THE WAKING SUN strewed shuttered gold upon the blue-gray waters of the silent river and the island air was filled with peace. Inside, in the echoing mansion Great Room, laughing young children were chasing one another while their parents, Paul and Christine Quandt, were in the library wrapping up some interesting business with a pair of tired Jesuit priests. One of them—husky, very young, inscrutable—stood with his hands in the pockets of his coat as he watched an older, taller priest tuck a book of prayers bound in bright red leather into a briefcase, snap it shut, and then scratch his nose with a freckled finger. "There, that's that," he sighed. "We're done."

He reached up and ran a hand through his thinning red hair.

Christine Quandt glanced into the Great Room.

"Oh, well, the kids are feeling good about the place," she noted.

The old priest followed her gaze. "Bless their hearts."

He picked up the briefcase.

A somber Paul Quandt was seated at the bar in a short-sleeved blue denim shirt and jeans. He shook his head. "I can't believe all this business started up again, Father."

"You moved back in when?" the priest asked him.

"May second. We'd been living in Europe. We'd taken the house off the market after that poor woman died, that realtor. My God, what a shock to come back to all this!"

He took a sip from a large white mug of coffee.

The red-haired Jesuit glanced to his companion, who'd continued to silently watch and wait. The young priest somberly and knowingly nodded and then fixed an unreadable gaze on Paul Quandt.

"Oh, well, yes, I can imagine," said the redheaded priest.

He moved toward the bar.

"Well, all right. And now let's hope that's the end of it," he offered.

"Really," Mrs. Quandt said dryly, nodding.

"I'll be waiting outside," the younger priest told the other with a move of his head. "I need a smoke."

"All right, Regis. Be right with you," the older man answered.

The young priest started away.

Paul Quandt called out to him.

"Thanks for everything, Father!"

"Me too!" his wife added.

The priest raised his hand in acknowledgment.

He kept walking and didn't look back.

"Good fellow," said the older priest, looking after him.

"So young," murmured Christine Quandt. She watched the young priest go out the door. "Looks barely twenty."

"Yes, I know," said the older man. "My assistant took suddenly ill; they found Regis at the very last minute for me."

"Oh, you just met at the house?"

"Yes, that's right." Something occurred to him. "Wasn't that the name of the boy who died? Your cousin? Edward Quandt's son?"

"Yes, it was," confirmed the wife.

"Lovely name."

The priest held out his hand.

"You won't stay for some brunch?" she asked.

"Thank you, no. I've got a mass at eleven. In the meantime, God bless," he said. "You're nice people." The priest took her hand. "Oh, would you please call the boatman?" he asked in an afterthought.

Paul Quandt got off the stool and shook his head.

"Already done it. Thanks again for the exorcism, Father."

"Well, let's hope that it gives you some peace."

Quandt nodded. "Amen."

"That's *my* line," said the priest.

The Quandts smiled. Then they noticed that the Jesuit was staring at something, a large oil painting above the fireplace of a man and a younger woman.

"Are these your famous aunt and uncle?"

Quandt said, "Yes."

The priest nodded, then said softly, "I know their story."

He slowly walked over to the painting, staring up.

"Tragic history: a murder and a suicide," he grieved.

"No," said Quandt quietly behind him.

The Jesuit turned around to him quizzically.

"No suicide," said Quandt.

"No suicide?"

Quandt came over and stood beside him, the porcelain coffee mug still in his grip. "No. No suicide, Father. Two murders."

"What?"

Quandt looked up at the man in the painting.

"Well, the truth of the matter, Father, is that Auntie apparently was cheating on Uncle and wanted him out of the way so badly that she put a deadly slow-acting poison in his drink. While he was dying, Uncle Edward found the vial that the poison had come in, and he sealed up Auntie alive in the crypt and then died himself right there on the spot."

"By the crypt?"

"By the crypt."

"How awful," said the priest.

"Not quite *Romeo and Juliet*," said Quandt.

His wife came up beside them. "Just misses."

The old priest took a final look at the painting, and then turned away to leave. "Well, I'll pray for them both."

"Thanks, Father," Paul Quandt told him. "I'd really like to imagine that they're at peace."

"Well, good-bye again."

The priest gave a wave.

"Bye, Father."

As the red-haired Jesuit left the room, a large collie dog came bounding up to him, and then followed him toward the door.

"Hello, boy," the priest greeted him.

"Oh, now, leave the good Father alone," Christine Quandt called out. "Come on, Tommy! Come on back here, you nutcase!"

The priest, still walking, looked over his shoulder. "No no no, I like dogs!" he called back. Then he turned and looked down at the collie. "Come on, Tommy! Good boy!"

The dog barked and leaped up at him playfully, following.

"Yes, I had a good doggie like you when I was little," said the priest. "Oh, yes, Tommy. Good boy. Good boy."

They had reached the entry hall. The priest opened the door and they went out. Paul Quandt put his arm around his wife's waist and together they looked up at the painting again. Riga Quandt had rugged, imperfect features that nevertheless were intensely sensual and gave an impression of beauty. Her star-crossed husband, Edward Quandt, had dark good looks, a chiseled face, and a vivid scar that jagged like lightning from his cheekbone down to the base of his jaw.

They were the faces of Morna and of Gabriel Case.

THE TWO PRIESTS and the dog were approaching the dock where the motor launch would soon pick them up. They could see it starting toward them from the opposite shore. The older priest picked up a stick and threw it. "Go, Tommy! Go!" he commanded. "Fetch!"

The dog took off with a bark and a bound.

The freckled old Jesuit glanced at the sky.

"Clearing up. Looks as if it's going to be a nice day."

They walked onto the dock and to its end, their steps thudding hollow on the dry old planks.

"I'm so glad you were able to fill in," said the older priest. "You're at Fordham, you said?"

"Yes, at Fordham."

"You know Father Bermingham there?"

The stolid priest shook his head.

"The directions were good, by the way? You found the village and the dock with no trouble?"

"No trouble. The launch was there waiting for me."

"Good. And so what do you think, young Regis? Tell me. Do you think we accomplished something? You believe the house is haunted?"

The other shook his head. "Beats me."

The old priest stared at him. "You look so young."

"I know."

The old man stared down at the sparkling waters where some blueness of the sky was beginning to reflect. "What a terrifying mystery the world presents to us, Regis. We know so little of the way things really are; of what *we* are, finally."

"True."

"A neutrino has no mass nor electrical charge and can pass through the planet in the twinkling of an eye. It's a ghost. And yet it's real, we know it's there, it exists. Ghosts are everywhere, I think; they're right beside us...lost souls...the unquiet dead. You know I wonder if..."

Turning to the Jesuit beside him, he broke off and looked puzzled, then taken aback. He looked around and behind him, frowning in bewilderment.

He said, "Regis?"

There was nobody there.